# L O N E
# S T A R
## on a
# C O W B O Y
# H E A R T

Lone Star on a Cowboy Heart
By Marie S. Crosswell

Published by Less Than Three Press LLC

Edited by Laura Garland
Cover designed by Natasha Snow

First Edition Month 2016
Copyright © 2016 by Marie S. Crosswell
Printed in the United States of America

Digital ISBN 9781620047903
Print ISBN 9781620047910

# LONE STAR

# on a

# COWBOY

# HEART

## Marie S. Crosswell

# CHAPTER ONE

*Prescott, Arizona*
*September 2014*

Sam Roswell stops for dinner at The Dog Bowl Diner in his civvies, his department-issued sidearm at home. He chats up his waitress because eating alone in public makes him lonely, and he doesn't have any friends in town yet. He watches the other people in the diner as he eats, feeling half *cop on the lookout for mischief* and half *looking for someone to meet*. There's a young family with a couple of restless kids who can't stay seated longer than a minute, an old husband and wife tucked into a two-person booth, three men and a woman side by side at the counter, and some teenagers hanging out. They're all on the opposite side of the diner, far enough away that everybody's within Sam's view.

Two men wearing black knit masks over their faces come in, each of them carrying a gun.

The man in a long-sleeved navy blue t-shirt moves into the populated section of the diner and says, "Everybody take out your wallets, now!"

The man wearing a dark red t-shirt under his jacket goes up to the counter and points his gun at the first employee he sees. "Open the register! Open it!"

The blonde waitress with big hair hurries to the register positioned at the right end of the counter and tries to obey, hands twitching and eyes panicked. Her first attempt fails.

"Hurry up!" Red Tee yells, steel revolver gleaming in the white lights screwed into the ceiling.

The register drawer clicks and slides open, and the waitress starts to yank the stacks of bills out of their compartments, dropping them on the countertop.

"Put the money in a bag! Put it in a fucking bag!"

She scrambles for the cash with one hand and clutches it as she looks around for the plastic take-out bags hooked onto the counter's interior. She finds them, tears one off, and sticks the money inside. Red Tee grabs it out of her hand and gives the bag to his accomplice, who shoves it at the family.

"Put your wallets in the fucking bag and pass it on," Blue Tee says to the room.

One of the children starts to cry in soft whimpers.

A boy sitting at the table of teenager's bolts for the door, but Red Tee gets hold of the hood on his sweatshirt and pulls him back.

"Where the fuck are you going?" Red Tee shouts, wrapping his free arm around the boy's neck and pressing his gun into the boy's head. "Huh?"

One of the teen girls yelps in horror.

Sam stands up and makes for Red Tee, plucking his badge off his belt as he goes. His pulse is fast, and waves of adrenaline start to wash through him. He's not thinking about what he's doing any more than he does when he drives a car, his body drawn to the trouble like a piece of metal to magnet.

"Hey, hey," he says, soft-spoken. He holds the badge in his hand before him, so everyone can see it. "Just calm down now. The kid's not going anywhere. Send him back to his seat, and you and your pal can get out of here."

"A cop, huh?" Red Tee says, arm still wrapped around the teenager's neck and the gun unrelenting on his skull. He raises his voice. "We got us a fucking cop in here."

Blue Tee glances over at Sam, still following the bag of money around his section of the diner as it changes hands.

"Where's your gun, asshole?" Red Tee says to Sam.

"Let the boy go," says Sam. "You got your money. You don't have to hurt anyone."

Red Tee stares at him through the eyehole in his mask, silent for a long beat, then shoves the teenager away from him. He points his gun at Sam's chest. "Maybe I'll kill you just to be on the safe side."

"He don't even have a fuckin' gun," says Blue Tee, the bag of money in his hand as he steps closer to the two other men. "Don't be stupid, let's just fucking go."

Sam's standing with his hands up in front of him, badge in the left and his right palm facing out.

Red Tee doesn't budge, staring him down with the revolver.

"I said, let's go," Blue Tee says, raising his voice.

"Fuck this cop," says Red Tee and cocks back the hammer on his revolver with his thumb.

BANG!

The right half of his skull blows apart in a spray of blood, bone, and brain, and he drops to the floor with his gun still in hand. A few of the women scream, and Sam flinches away and covers his head with his arms, then looks again at where Red Tee had been standing.

A tall man who Sam didn't notice earlier comes down the path splitting the diner in half, leading to the bathrooms in the back, aiming a pistol in his right hand at Blue Tee. He's lean and long-limbed, a wavy lock of dark hair hanging over his forehead, eyes gray and hard like stone.

"You motherfucker!" Blue Tee yells, looking at his dead accomplice bleeding on the tile and aiming his own gun at the stranger.

"I wouldn't if I were you," the stranger says, his voice dark and slow like raw maple syrup. An accent that could be Texas or mid-South. "This cop here is going to call his buddies now. The sooner you get, better chance you have of not being found. Or I can kill you. Save them the trouble of chasing after you."

Blue Tee looks at him, hesitating, the bag of money still clutched in his hand.

The stranger blinks at him, lazy and calm.

Blue Tee runs out of the diner.

Sam follows him as he hears the engine in a vehicle start, watches as the pick-up truck squeals out of the lot and down the road southbound. The red taillights glow and fade into the night.

He goes back inside, his nerves frayed. Somebody, a woman or a kid, is crying.

The stranger looks across the diner at Sam, unruffled, dark eyes slanted, and says, "What's a sheriff's deputy doing without his gun?"

Sam swallows and doesn't answer. The truth would sound stupid.

The stranger looks over at the blonde waitress cowering behind the counter. "Better call 911," he says.

She picks up the old landline phone attached to the wall near the kitchen doorway, like she needed someone to tell her what to do. When she starts talking to the emergency operator, her voice sounds like it's been shredded through a grater, high-pitched and borderline hysterical.

The stranger makes for the door, stepping over Red Tee's corpse in his cowboy boots like the dead man's a puddle of spilt milk. He tucks his gun into the holster on the back of his waistband and passes Sam without another word or look.

Sam doesn't think to stop him.

# CHAPTER TWO

Two weeks go by, before Sam sees the stranger at The Bird Cage Saloon, drinking alone at the end of the bar. He doesn't notice him until after the people sitting between them leave. He's into his first beer and looks over to his right. He almost doesn't believe it. Nobody could tell Sam who the stranger was when he asked around, after the shooting. Not the sheriff or other deputies, not the diner employees, nor any of their friends and family. Sam resigned himself to the likelihood that the stranger didn't live in the area and was probably gone for good, back to whatever state gave him that accent. He didn't have a signature on a receipt or a license plate number. All he had was the slug dug out of Red Tee's body.

The stranger's wearing a black cowboy hat, hunched over with his arms resting on the bar top and his boot heels hooked over the lowest rung of his stool. He's thinking about something or maybe nothing at all, listening to the bluesy country song playing through the speakers.

Sam gets up, taking his beer bottle with him. He's slow to approach the stranger, like he's coming up on a rabbit or a deer that's sure to run away if he isn't careful. He stops at the stranger's left shoulder, pauses, and says, "Hey."

The stranger turns his head to look at him, and his eyes brighten with surprise.

"I'm Sam Roswell, the sheriff's deputy from The Dog Bowl."

"Yeah, you are," says the stranger.

"It's good to see you again," Sam says. "It's been bothering me ever since that night, not being able to thank you—for saving my life. Probably the lives of the other people there, too."

The stranger shakes his head. "I don't need to be thanked."

"Well, you gotta let me buy you a drink. I insist." Sam sits on the stool next to the stranger. "I never found out who you are," he says, after a moment.

The stranger doesn't answer at first. "Name's Montgomery. Montgomery Clarke."

"You're not from around here, are you?"

"No, sir. I live in Skull Valley. From South Texas, originally."

"Skull Valley," says Sam. "I've never been."

"Well," says Montgomery, "not much there worth seeing. Ranches and farms, mostly. Windmills."

"Do you own one? A ranch?"

"Nope. I'm just a hand. I work Bill Barbee's ranch."

Montgomery drains his beer and sets the bottle down across the bar. He makes eye contact with the bartender, who comes over to him.

"Another one?" the bartender says.

"Make it a whiskey," Montgomery says. "Bulleit, please."

"I'm buying," says Sam.

The bartender pours a couple shots of Bulleit into a lowball glass and passes it to Montgomery.

"Anything for you?" he asks Sam.

11

"Another beer, please."

The bartender moves back down to the other end of the bar for the cooler and comes back with an uncapped bottle of the beer Sam's drinking.

Sam waits until he's out of earshot again to say, "You haven't asked about the men in the diner."

Montgomery sips on his whiskey, eyes climbing up and down the wall behind the bar. "Maybe because I'm not interested."

Sam fidgets on his stool and finishes his beer, trading the empty bottle for the second. "The man you shot was Ed Decker, from Dewey-Humboldt," Sam says, lowering his voice. "He had a wife and three kids. I went down there to talk to her, after she identified the body. It sounds like they were having some financial difficulties."

Montgomery doesn't reply, taking another sip from his glass.

"The other man, the one who got away, is Joel Troutman—one of Decker's friends. We only know that because he's been missing since the morning of the hold-up, according to his wife. So he's our best bet." Sam pauses, remembering the women's faces. "They needed the money and didn't know what else to do. They must've thought that holding up a place in Prescott was safer than doing it in their own town."

"You feel sorry for'em," says Montgomery. "I don't."

Sam looks at him. "I can hold them accountable for what they did wrong and still have compassion."

"You're talking about at least one man who was ready to kill you, just for the satisfaction of it. Plenty of people got money troubles. Most of them don't rob other people at gunpoint. Now, they've left their families worse off, without their earning power. Stupid."

Sam can't argue with him, so he doesn't.

They're silent for a little while, Sam's elbow scraping against Montgomery's every time he lifts his drink to his mouth and lowers it again. It's half an hour to closing time and not too many people linger behind them and beside them at the bar. Prescott's a quiet town on weeknights, when the tourists are few and the residents are in bed before midnight on account of work or old age. The bartender's already wiping down the bar, at the other end, a heavyset man with a bald head and black mustache.

"The sheriff's office would appreciate it if you came in to give your statement," says Sam. "About what happened at the diner."

"Is that why you're sitting here talking to me?" Montgomery says.

"No."

"You know what happened. So do the two dozen other people who were there."

"You killed a man. It's not unreasonable for the sheriff to want a conversation with you. Anyway, I'm pretty sure he wants to shake your hand. Congratulate you for being a hero."

"I'm not a God damn hero. Nobody knows what the hell that word means."

Sam pauses and drinks, before changing the subject. "You live on the ranch where you work?" he says.

"No," says Montgomery. "I got my own place. Little house not far from Barbee's."

"I'm guessing you come to Prescott to eat and drink sometimes, on account of there not being too many options in your neck of the woods."

"You guess right."

"Do you always carry a gun like that?"

"It's registered."

"I don't know why a cowboy living in the boonies would need that kind of hardware."

"Snakes, cougars, and would-be cop killers. There's three."

Sam can't hold back a half-grin as he dips his head to drink.

They fall back into quiet for a while, sitting side by side like they're old friends used to companionable silence, ignoring the rest of the room. A few more people pick up their jackets and leave.

Sam checks his watch. "Don't you get up early for work?" he says.

Montgomery looks at him. "Don't you?"

"Probably not as early as a ranch hand."

Montgomery looks away. "Tomorrow's my day off."

Sam nods and doesn't speak again for a minute or two, looking in the mirror at the hazy reflection of multi-colored string lights wrapped around the antlers of taxidermied moose and deer heads mounted on the wall. A few more stare blank-eyed directly above the men. Sam looks at himself sitting next to Montgomery, hazel eyes darkened in the dimness of the saloon. Montgomery has his head bowed, his face hidden under the brim of his hat, so Sam appraises himself the way he usually does in the privacy of his bathroom at home.

Since moving to Prescott, he's allowed his facial hair to grow in, though it's too short to count for a beard. He's not sure why. Maybe it's part of starting over, changing himself as much as his life. His dark blonde hair is cut so short that he can barely run his fingers through it, messy on top and buzzed close to the scalp on the sides. He's almost pale compared to Montgomery, who's tan from working outside every day. When he's off duty like this, dressed in civilian clothes, he blends right in with the Prescott locals. Not bad-looking but not someone who stands out either.

Montgomery lifts his head, his face appearing next to Sam's. He probably could've been a model in another life, though he's too old for it now. "So tell me, Deputy," he says. "Why didn't you have your gun in that diner?"

Sam drops his gaze to the bar top and pauses. "I don't like carrying it around when I'm off duty," he says. "Never have. Maybe it's stupid of me to leave it at home, but.... I feel better when I don't have to worry about it."

Montgomery doesn't reply, just lifts his glass to his lips and drinks more whiskey.

"Why didn't you do something sooner?" Sam says.

"What do you mean?" says Montgomery.

"At the diner. Why didn't you step in sooner—try to stop the robbery?"

Montgomery doesn't answer for a moment, peering down at the last sliver of whiskey in the bottom of his glass. "I was hoping they'd take their money and go, I guess. Didn't want to make a bad situation worse."

15

"Guns tend to do that," Sam concedes. "You know, I didn't even see you there before you fired."

"Did you comb the whole building before sittin' down?"

"No."

The bartender comes back to the two men and says, "Closing time, fellas."

They dig their wallets out of back pockets. Sam leaves enough cash for his two beers and Montgomery's whiskey.

They step out into the chilly night air and stand on the sidewalk with the saloon door at their backs. The street's quiet, stars white and thick above the trees in the town square and the Yavapai County Courthouse.

Montgomery lights up a cigarette just as Sam turns to shake his hand.

"Thank you," Sam says. "I'd probably be dead if it wasn't for you."

A hint of bashfulness crosses Montgomery's mouth, and he nods, taking Sam's hand and shaking it.

"Please consider stopping by the station here in town to give your statement."

"I'll think about it," Montgomery says. "Good night, Deputy."

"Night."

Sam watches as Montgomery walks down Whiskey Row to his truck, the other man's silhouette like the shape of something in a dream.

\*~\*~\*

A week passes, and if Montgomery talks to

anyone at the Sheriff's station in Prescott, Sam doesn't hear about it. He gets into his car early on a Saturday morning and drives west out of town, taking Iron Springs Road through the forest hills before it bends southbound back into desert. It takes him twenty minutes to reach the intersection where Skull Valley's only businesses stand: a garage and gas station, a general store, a post office, a diner, an elementary school, a fire station, and a church. The streets are deserted, but there are several vehicles parked at the diner and a couple more in front of the general store.

Sam pulls up to the old garage, painted mustard yellow with vintage red gas pumps from the '50s. He parks the car and goes inside the service room. A woman is sitting behind the counter reading a magazine, and music plays through an old portable radio set on the counter. The woman looks up at Sam and smiles.

"Hello, how can I help you?" she says.

"Hi," he says. "I was wondering if you could help me find someone. He lives around here somewhere. I don't have an address."

"Sure, who you looking for?"

"Montgomery Clarke? He works on the Barbee ranch?"

She nods. "He's tall and quiet, always wears a cowboy hat. I remember him. I don't think we've seen him in here for a little while. A few weeks, maybe. You know, folks like to take gas to go, especially if they live out a ways. Why don't I go ask my husband if he knows where to find him."

She gets up and disappears into the back, going through the door connected to the garage. She comes back a couple minutes later and says, "I'm sorry, but he doesn't know where Mr. Clarke lives, either. You might have better luck at the cafe. Ask Aaron, the manager. He knows the community pretty well."

Sam walks to the Skull Valley Diner. The small dining room is packed, every table and counter seat taken by families, couples, ranchers, and old bikers whose Harleys are parked right outside. Sunlight streams through the wide windows, their threadbare lace curtains drawn open. Forest green pleather chairs line the long, low counter made of polished blonde wood, and the wall behind the counter plated with the same wood is covered in black and white photographs of Skull Valley ranchers and cowboys from decades back. The only decoration on the diner's white walls are a few framed prints of cowboy paintings. The doors and windows are lined with green trim that match the counter seats. One young waitress with long red hair in a ponytail moves easily across the tiled floor, dropping off coffees, checking on every party, and making small talk. She sees Sam and beelines for him. Her nametag, pinned to her uniform front, says *Joy*.

"Welcome to the Skull Valley Diner, sir. It's going to be about a fifteen to twenty minute wait for inside seating, or you can place an order to go."

"Actually, I want to talk to your manager. Aaron?"

She looks a little alarmed. "Oh. Okay. Let me go get him."

She heads into the kitchen, then comes out again and goes to the first door on the right in the short corridor leading to the back of the diner. She knocks, speaks to the person inside, and a man emerges behind her as she returns to the main floor. He's tall and burly, with a short, thick beard, and he's wearing a red flannel shirt tucked into his belted jeans. His arms and shoulders bulge in the sleeves. He looks like a lumberjack, not a guy who spends his days managing a diner. He approaches Sam and holds out a big hand to shake when he's close enough.

"Morning," he says. "I'm Aaron; how can I help you?"

Sam shakes with him. "I'm Sam Roswell. The garage told me you might know where Montgomery Clarke lives. I'm looking for him."

"Clarke."

"Yeah, he's a ranch hand—wears a black cowboy hat, quiet, probably comes in alone."

"Right." Aaron, hands on his hips now, looks at the floor for a moment. "Sir, I have to be honest with you, people respect each other's privacy around here, and I'm not too comfortable with the idea of giving a stranger my customer's address, not knowing what your intentions are."

"I understand," Sam says. He moves the right side of his jacket open to show off his deputy star clipped to his belt. "I'm with the Yavapai County Sheriff's. I just need to talk to him about something."

The suspicion dissolves out of Aaron's face, replaced with slight surprise. "Let me write you directions."

The house, like most others in Skull Valley, is at the end of a dirt drive off the nearest paved road.

Sam has to turn around and go back north from the town center, then east past a handful of other homesteads that don't look much like ranches or anything else. He has to count the lot entrances he passes to make sure he finds the right one, because there is nothing to mark addresses on the street, not even individual mailboxes.

When he hits the right number, he turns into the dirt path, this one much shorter than those leading to ranch estates on bigger lots. He's relieved when he sees the house exactly as the cafe manager described in the notes: an unpainted wood cabin with a raised porch and a stone chimney built into the back like a spine. The door and the roofline are painted pine green, and there's an old pickup truck parked at a diagonal in front, nose pointing at the corner of the porch on the right. It's a 1985 black Chevy Silverado with silver trim, covered in dust and sandy colored dirt caking the tires.

Sam climbs up the porch steps, pauses, and knocks on the door light-handed.

After a moment of silence, Montgomery opens up. He looks less intimidating without his hat on, but he's still about six foot four in his cowboy boots. He looks at Sam with a hint of surprise. "Deputy," he says, "what are you doing here?"

Sam now realizes this is not usually how a man makes a friend. "You still haven't submitted your statement about the diner robbery to the sheriff's."

Montgomery pauses, raising his arm to rest against the inside of the doorjamb and leaning his weight on that leg. "Don't ya'll have a secretary makes phone calls? If you can track down where I live, you could've got my number."

"I had a hunch you'd ignore it if we did call."

Montgomery stands there for a beat, holding the door open, the same somber but unreadable expression on his face that he wore the first two times Sam saw him. "You can come in," he says, stepping backward into the house.

Sam follows him inside.

The living room is almost Spartan in its decor, which tells Sam that what little decoration there is must have personal meaning to Montgomery. A long, green leather couch is pushed against the front wall of the house, below the window to the left of the door. There's a knit Navajo blanket spread across half of the couch, accented with one dented pillow. In front of the couch, there's a low-standing coffee table with nothing but a dirty ashtray on it, one thick, smooth slab of dark wood on short legs. A rifle, clean and polished, is mounted on the wall to the left of the kitchen entrance, and a steer skull hangs on the wall to the right. A portable heater is plugged into an outlet behind the far end of the couch.

Opposite the couch, there are two easy chairs, one chocolate brown leather and the other olive green cloth. Behind the chairs on the floor is a colorful area rug with faded edges that looks Mexican made. A bookcase full of books stands in the corner opposite the couch. There are coat hooks installed in the wall next to the door, two of them taken by Montgomery's black cowboy hat and a denim jacket. Below them are boots standing neat on the floor, one cowboy pair and one pair of lace-up work shoes, both of them dirty and well-worn.

No television. No photographs.

"You want coffee?" Montgomery says, heading into the kitchen.

"Yeah," says Sam, "Coffee would be good."

"How do you take it?"

"Just cream."

Montgomery disappears, and Sam sits on the couch, uneasy—like he isn't supposed to be there.

Montgomery comes back with two mugs and offers one to Sam. Before letting him have it, he looks at him and says, "I ain't giving you a statement." He turns around and sits in the brown chair, smelling the coffee without drinking it yet.

"Why not?" Sam says.

"You were there. You saw what happened. I don't have to tell it to you."

Before he can mention it as a justification for giving testimony, Sam remembers that Montgomery already explained his actions at the diner when they spoke in the saloon. "Guess I can write the statement myself and hand it to the sheriff." He tests his coffee with a ginger sip.

Montgomery's looking out the window behind Sam, and the sunlight sharpens the color of his eyes. Hazel green. Slate. Earth colors.

"How'd you know I'd be home?" he says.

"I didn't," says Sam. "How many days off you get?"

"Two. Sometimes three. Guess you could say I'm part-time, in ranching terms. Bill's got plenty of hands younger'n me happy to be there six or seven days a week, and I don't need the money that bad. But I like to stay busy."

Montgomery drinks some of his coffee.

"What do you do, exactly?" Sam asks.

22

"A lot of things," says Montgomery. "Most of it amounts to looking after horses and cattle. There's the occasional maintenance job. I've done plenty of teaching to the younger hands. First timers. Bill appreciates not having to do it himself."

They're quiet for a couple minutes, sipping from their mugs.

"You ain't been here long, have you?" Montgomery says, looking at Sam.

"I moved from California a few months ago," says Sam. "I was with Lassen County Sheriff's Department up north."

"Why the hell'd you come to Prescott, Arizona?"

Sam just looks at him, eyes sliding down into his coffee as he chooses not to answer.

Montgomery doesn't push.

"How did you end up here?" Sam asks him.

"I was in Tucson for a while. Decided I wanted a change of scenery." Montgomery stretches out his long legs, crossing them at the ankles, and slouches into his chair. "You any closer to finding your fugitive?"

"Joel Troutman. No."

"He's probably long gone with that money," says Montgomery. "If he's smart."

"His wife's still in Dewey-Humboldt."

"Giving up a wife's one thing. Giving up your freedom's something else."

Sam looks at him and doesn't reply. The sun coming through the window behind him is warm across his shoulders and his bare neck. "You live alone, I take it," he says.

"Last I checked," says Montgomery. "You?"

Sam nods. "Yeah. I came by myself."

They fall silent again for a long few minutes, drinking their coffee, never looking at each other at the same time. The house is quiet, not even the sound of wind against the wood or the windowpanes.

"How long have you been in Skull Valley?" Sam says.

"Four years," says Montgomery.

"Why did you decide to live here instead of Prescott?"

"Fewer people, the better."

Sam doesn't understand the appeal of isolation, so he finishes his coffee instead of responding. He wants to know if Montgomery has any friends at all, but he can't think of a good way to ask that question.

"You should put up wanted posters," Montgomery says.

"What?" says Sam.

"For Troutman."

"Right. Maybe."

Montgomery sits up, leans forward, and sets his mug on the table. He stands, digging into his back pocket for a lighter. "I need a smoke," he says.

Sam gets up and follows him outside. They stand at the top of the porch steps, even though there's one rocking chair behind them. Montgomery lights a cigarette, draws on it, and exhales with a long sigh of satisfaction. Sam's got his empty mug in between both hands like an excuse for being here.

"You know people in Prescott?" he says.

"Not really," says Montgomery, looking out at the landscape. "The dead man's wife—she ask who killed him?"

Sam looks at him. "No. I don't think she cares."

Montgomery's quiet for a beat, bowing his head and scraping his boot on the step, then looking up again. His face doesn't give anything away. "What'd you say his name was?"

"Decker. Ed Decker."

Montgomery smokes for a minute without speaking. "Tell me something, Deputy. Why'd you pick law enforcement?"

Sam blinks at Montgomery. Nobody's asked him that question in years. He hasn't thought about it in as long either. "I wanted to do something with my life that mattered, I guess. And I probably thought, when I was younger, that it'd be exciting. Why did you go into ranching?"

"Whatever keeps a man close to nature beats just about anything else, I reckon. There's a satisfaction in going home and feeling worked. If I'm going to sit on my ass all day, I might as well be dead."

Sam smiles, not without feeling a twinge of shame in his gut about all the hours he spends sitting at a desk or in his car when in uniform.

Montgomery takes one last draw on his cigarette, now smoked to the filter. "Good luck forging my statement," he says.

Sam takes it as his cue to leave. "Thanks," he says, offering his empty mug to the other man.

Montgomery takes it and drops his cigarette butt inside.

Sam nods and starts down the steps with his fingers shoved into his pockets and a sense of disappointment. He must be lonelier than he realized.

"Hey," Montgomery calls, when Sam's halfway to his car.

Sam looks back.

"You know how to ride?"

"A horse, you mean?"

"What else?"

Sam pauses. "I'm rusty. "

Montgomery looks at him. "Snoop your way to the Barbee ranch next Saturday, nine in the AM. We'll see how rusty you are."

He turns around and goes back into the house, the screen door slapping against the jamb behind him.

Sam smiles.

# CHAPTER THREE

Montgomery drives out to Dewey-Humboldt on his next day off, not thinking too hard about why. He stops at the only place in town worth being in: Billy Jack's Saloon, a standalone dive on the side of Highway 69. There are a few vehicles parked in front and alongside of the small building, even at eleven o'clock in the morning. A tall metal pole stands outside the saloon with a red COORS sign hanging to the side at the top and another sign reading BILLY JACK'S SALOON with images of a beer mug and a redhead shooting pool. Wire fence encloses a narrow area of outside seating right next to the front door, and multi-colored big bulb string lights line the roof edges. Part of the saloon's south side is nothing but exposed wooden boards.

Inside, the bar is on the right, and the pool tables and extra seating are on the left. The ceiling above the bar is covered in dollar bills glued on with signatures and messages scrawled in black marker. Neon light signs for Budweiser, Tecate, Coors Light, and Jack Daniel's Original Hard Cola glow red and green on the walls. There's a small TV mounted in the left corner behind the bar and another one on the back wall of the saloon opposite the entrance, the older box models instead of flat screens.

Montgomery sits near the middle of the bar, wearing his black cowboy hat.

The bartender, a stocky man in his forties with a

fringe of pepper hair lining his jaw and upper lip, comes over. "Haven't seen you in a while," he says.

"Here I am," says Montgomery. "How are you?"

"Fine. What'll you have?"

"Cold beer would be good. Bottled."

The bartender pulls a beer out of the cooler and pops off the cap before setting it in front of Montgomery.

"Thanks," Montgomery says and starts sipping.

They don't speak for a few minutes. The bar is quiet enough that they can hear the football game on TV, and the bartender turns his back on Montgomery to watch it.

"Hey," he says, voice low and smoker's raspy.

The bartender faces him again.

"You ever serve a man in here by the name of Joel Troutman?"

"Maybe. Tell me what he looks like and I might remember."

Montgomery saw a photograph of Troutman on the local news just last night, on Bill Barbee's TV. Either the bartender didn't watch the broadcast or he's playing dumb. Troutman was presented as a missing person from Dewey, not as the runaway suspect who survived the diner hold-up in Prescott. He figures the sheriff's department wants Troutman to think that they haven't identified him as their fugitive. He gives the bartender the description he heard on the news.

"He's under six foot, dark hair, little bit more on the face than you. Between thirty-five and forty years old. Average build, kinda broad in the shoulders. He's married. Drives a blue Ford pick-up."

The bartender creases his face in concentration.

"I think he works construction," Montgomery adds.

"I might know who you're talking about," says the bartender.

"You mighta seen him come in with Ed Decker, if that helps."

"Shit. I do know who you're talking about. Joel, yeah, he did come with Ed a few times." The bartender leans down toward Montgomery and lowers his voice. "Ed Decker's dead. Something happened to him a few weeks ago. Bunch of rumors are going around."

Montgomery drinks some of his beer, not reacting beyond a sleepy-eyed blink.

"What do you want to know about Joel Troutman for?"

"What can you tell me about him?" Montgomery asks.

The bartender looks at him with his mouth pressed into a tight line, maybe hesitant or unsure. "You said Troutman's married, right?"

Montgomery nods.

"Pretty sure he come in apart from Ed sometimes, with a woman named Donna. She's a blonde. Got a nice rack. Only, she don't wear a wedding ring... and times Joel showed up here with Ed and Ed's wife, he was with a brunette."

Montgomery raises his chin and his eyebrows, swirling the base of his beer bottle above the bar top. "Troutman's been screwing around. Hmm."

The bartender looks guilty for tattling, face now speckled with perspiration. "Anyway, that's about the only thing I can think of," he says.

"You know Donna's last name?" Montgomery asks. "Or somebody who does?"

The bartender shakes his head. "No. But I got something else."

He walks off to the cash register at the end of the bar, opens the drawer, lifts the money organizer and pulls something out from under it. He comes back and pushes it across the bar top with his forefinger.

A crumpled, dirty paper napkin with a phone number written on it.

Montgomery looks up at him. "You know this is hers?"

"Yeah. She left it for someone, when she was here alone once. He didn't take it."

Montgomery sticks the napkin into his hip pocket and nods. "Thanks."

The bartender nods and leaves him alone, returning to the back end of the bar.

Montgomery nurses his beer, listening to the soft noises of the television and people talking behind him, and circles around the question of what he's doing. He doesn't want to get too close, doesn't want to touch it with his hands, but he's aware of the question, even more than that now—attentive. He's got no reason to care where the fugitive Joel Troutman is or where he goes with that sack of money. It's sure as hell not his job to find him.

But here he is.

He can name all the things this isn't about. It isn't an irrational fear that Troutman will come back to avenge Ed Decker. It isn't guilt over killing a man. It isn't any kind of heroic urge begging to see Troutman brought to justice for the robbery, and it isn't a rotten pulse of greed hankering for the hold-up spoils. It isn't about Troutman at all, if he's honest.

Montgomery drains the beer bottle and leaves a five on the bar, before walking back out into the bleached daylight. He stands in the parking lot and lights a cigarette, watching the highway and the landscape on the other side of it. Tries to imagine Decker and Troutman scheming the robbery inside the saloon, drinking one night just the two of them, tossing around the idea without meaning it yet.

He wonders if they were close.

He doesn't think they were.

*~*~*

Sam gives himself an extra half hour to find the Barbee Ranch, and he uses about twenty minutes of it, after asking for directions at the Skull Valley General Store. The ranch is on the western side of Iron Springs Road and north of the town center, past a handful of other homesteads. Sam follows a skinny paved road branching off Iron Springs, then takes a couple dirt paths to the main entrance of Barbee's property, marked with a sign in the metal archway above the gate reading BLITHE BEE RANCH. He drives in and sees Montgomery standing in the middle of the long, wide, unpaved driveway with his arms crossed and the back end of his pickup truck behind him. Sam parks his car and gets out, Carhartt work boots scraping at the gravel. He's wearing his lined denim jacket, because he'd rather be too warm than cold for however long Montgomery's going to keep him on horseback.

"You're on time," Montgomery says, as Sam approaches him. "I was going to give you a half hour to be late finding the place."

"It's not that hard to find with directions," says Sam, without mentioning that Montgomery never offered any.

"Hope you had breakfast. 'round here, lunch is about noon."

The dirt drive winds past Montgomery's pick-up and reaches far back into the property. The main house, where the Barbees live, is off to the left behind Montgomery. The ranch style home is long and low to the ground, painted white with forest green window and door trim, the roof's wood shingles a dark, earthy brown. The front porch is covered and decorated with a few large potted plants, and there's a rocking bench seat near the front door.

Montgomery leads Sam around the house and across a grassy backyard to a big barn, its double doors already wide open. Sam waits for him as he disappears into the first stall on the right and reemerges leading a horse that's already been saddled and bridled.

"This one's yours for the day," he tells Sam.

The horse is a dark chocolate brown, almost black, with a well-kept blonde mane and tail. He's never seen a horse with her colors before, and he's struck by how pleasing she is to look at. Her body is slender with graceful lines, and she has a kind face, black eyes peering at Sam with a look that he recognizes from various women he's known: a combination of gentle concern and curiosity.

"Her name's Cavendish," Montgomery says,

handing him the reins. "Rocky Mountain breed, something special Bill gave his wife. Just about the easiest thing to ride around here."

Sam raises his hand to her nose and lets her sniff his palm. "Mrs. Barbee won't mind me taking her?" he says.

"Nope."

Montgomery disappears into the stall across from Cavendish's and comes out leading a buckskin Quarter Horse. Like Sam's, the horse is already saddled and bridled. The body is custard yellow, and the mane and tail are black, along with the horse's ankles. Color wise, this horse appears to be the inverse of Sam's. It has a masculine, handsome face and a thicker, stronger frame than Sam's mare. It might be the most beautiful animal Sam's ever seen, and just a minute ago, he thought that honor belonged to Cavendish.

"This is Gold Dust," says Montgomery. "Best all-around stock horse in Barbee's stable."

He looks at the horse with a trace of affection in his eyes, the slightest smile on his lips, holding the reins in one hand. It's the first time Sam's seen him pleased by something, and he now realizes that if he's going to understand and grow close to this man, he'll have to learn to appreciate these animals.

Without being asked, Montgomery moves to hold Cavendish steady, so Sam can mount her. It's been years since Sam got on a horse, and he's tentative when he sticks his right foot into the stirrup. Montgomery withholds instruction. Sam hauls his weight up onto the mare in one fluid motion, swinging his left leg over her and settling in the saddle. He forgot how high up he'd be. He's not quite ready for Montgomery to hand over the reins and let go of Cavendish, but he doesn't object. Montgomery hops onto Gold Dust and without a word, rides out of the barn ahead of Sam.

Sam follows him. It doesn't feel like he's riding the horse—more like the horse is taking him along with her.

Barbee's homestead is a hundred acres of deeded land, most of it pasture for the horses, paired with five thousand acres of surrounding state land allotted for livestock grazing. With seven horses and fifty-five head of cattle, the ranch is a small operation, one that the Barbees chose for their retirement after decades on a much bigger ranch in southeastern Arizona. Headquarters on the deeded land consists of the main house, horse barn, working corrals, garage, storage shed, tack room, and shop. None of the ranch hands live on the property, but there are a couple mobile homes situated at a distance from the back of the main house, used when workers need to stay overnight. Montgomery explains to Sam that the Barbees plan on selling off the cattle when they can no longer take care of them and hold onto some of the horses.

"You ever think about getting your own?" Sam asks, as they amble through an open pasture of yellow grass, riding west.

"When I was younger, I thought about it," Montgomery says. "At some point, I realized that loving the work doesn't mean I want to deal with the responsibility of ownership. Or the commitment. Owning things—it ties you down, makes it hard to move on to somewhere else should you care to."

The grazing pastures stretch the length of a football field behind the Barbee's house, fenced apart from it and a patch of yard saved for grandchildren and their brightly colored playsets. Those pastures open up into wider fields that lead into wilderness, and the fencing disappears from sight in the back of the homestead, reaching far west along the front and the dirt road running parallel. A few of the other horses are scattered throughout the field, long necks sloping to the ground as they nibble on grass, heads lifting to watch the two men riding past them. Montgomery stays ahead of Sam by one horse length, and Sam can tell that he's setting the pace slow to ease him into riding.

They sit the horses at the edge of a plateau that slopes off into another stretch of plains several feet below and look around at Barbee's land, at the treetops brushing the bottom of the sky and the mountains far beyond them. They breathe in the clear, cool air and don't say a word for a long time, a single bird crying the only sound they can hear. The landscape has more color and beauty out here than in the other parts of Skull Valley Sam saw, including Montgomery's own little homestead. It feels like they're a thousand miles from civilization, even this close to the ranch house, and Sam doesn't have a hard time imagining a solitary man disappearing into this space. His sheriff deputy work, the hunt for Joel Troutman, a world of robberies and murders might as well belong to someone else now.

Sam glances over at Montgomery's left hand resting on his thigh, notices the bare ring finger.

"You ever been married?" he asks.

Montgomery squints into the distance, his face tanned to a peachy brown from so much time spent outside. He's quiet for a long time. "Once," he says.

Sam can't tell if there's anything in his voice like regret or nostalgia. He looks away, in the same direction as Montgomery and says, "Me and my ex-wife were together for six years, total. Married four."

"What was her name?"

Sam looks at him again, almost surprised at the show of interest. "Jen."

"Jen Roswell," Montgomery says, like he sees her out there, somewhere on the horizon line.

"Not anymore," says Sam, with just a touch of wistfulness.

"When'd you split?"

"About a year ago."

Montgomery looks over at him. "So that's why you moved to Prescott. Ran away from her."

"I didn't run away," says Sam. "We lived in a small town. I thought it'd be easier on her if I left."

Montgomery turns his eyes back to the landscape and doesn't argue.

"What about you?" Sam asks, after a minute. "What was her name?"

"Annalee." Montgomery speaks the name like it's something he put on a shelf and hasn't touched in a long time. "Al for short."

Sam nods. Cavendish flicks her ears.

"What's she look like?" Sam says.

Montgomery smirks and shakes his head. "Good enough for a man to make bad decisions. But it didn't make much difference to me what she looked like."

Sam frowns in confusion.

Montgomery starts his horse forward before Sam can ask him to explain.

They ride down the slope and across another open pasture, continuing into a thicket of cottonwood trees that have yellowed for the season. It's a little warmer now, the sun brighter in the sky.

Sam thinks about his ex-wife as he keeps his eyes on Montgomery's back. Jen is a real estate agent with long, blonde hair. They met in a country western bar, one night in Susanville, California—the Lassen County seat. She asked him for a dance, and he surprised her with how good he was. She's an outdoorsy woman, like most people in California. She hikes, jogs, and goes four wheeling. When they lived together, she would go on long bike rides, weekend mornings. She never asked Sam to go with her. He never wanted to.

It's strange what you remember about someone gone from your life. Jen almost never painted her nails, but when she did, she always picked robin's egg blue. She played on her high school softball team all four years but not in college. She has a raised scar about four inches long, starting at the base of her neck on the left side and angling down toward her shoulder blade at a diagonal. She's wanted a tattoo since she was fifteen, but she could never decide what to get. Her lips were always soft; she used a lot of lip balm but rarely wore lipstick. When she tanned, the freckles surfaced across her face like a dash of cinnamon in a cup of milky coffee.

Either Montgomery slows his horse or Sam speeds up, but they come alongside each other somehow, riding in silence for a few minutes more.

"You think you'll get married again?" Sam asks, blurting out the question the second it occurs to him.

"Hell, no," says Montgomery. "Didn't agree with me the first time."

"Why not?"

Montgomery glances at Sam and doesn't answer.

They ride under the cottonwood trees until they arrive at another clearing, where the mountains reappear in the distance, blue and impenetrable, following the horizon line as far as they can see. A few cows, two black and one brown, stand scattered before them.

"You mind if I give this horse a run?" Montgomery asks.

"No," Sam says, looking over at him.

Montgomery nods and knocks his heels into his horse's sides, speeding up into a fast trot. He's yards ahead in a minute or two, and Sam watches him, picturing Montgomery out here alone, day in and day out. He fits the scenery too well, the lone cowboy who's half-wild animal himself, as good as caged at somebody's dining room table with the forks on the left and the knives on the right. Sam wonders if anybody really knows Montgomery, if Sam can know him or if he's too used to this silent relationship with nature to allow for human closeness. Maybe it's a futile endeavor, trying to befriend a man like this one, but Sam wants to try. He wants to tread the bottom of the well.

Montgomery rides in a wide arch, from right to left, coming back around toward Sam. The cows don't flinch or flee as he passes them, knowing when to respond to horseback riders and when to ignore them. Sam runs his hand along the side of his horse's neck, feeling her body respond to him, and watches as Montgomery returns.

They continue on, silent again, walking the horses about as slow as they can go.

Montgomery drapes the reins across his saddle and digs his lighter and a cigarette out of his shirt pocket. He lights up and says, "What about you? You looking to find wife number two?"

"I don't know," Sam says, the answer more thoughtful than the question. "I don't know what I want now. I thought I was going to be married to Jen forever."

Montgomery slips his lighter back in his pocket and smokes. The corners of his mouth quirk up, smile dying before it forms.

"What?"

Montgomery turns his head toward Sam, eyes weathered. "Forever's a lie only people can tell themselves," he says.

He holds the cigarette in his fingers and looks out ahead into the landscape again, smoke squiggling away from his hand.

Sam watches him longer than he should. He wonders if Montgomery really is that cynical. Wonders about Montgomery's ex-wife, the kind of woman it takes to wrangle a man like that into marriage. He wants to ask why they split, whose idea it was, if Montgomery hates her or loves her. He holds his tongue because they don't know each other well enough, and Montgomery strikes him as a private man.

They ride deeper into the wilderness, through a grove of black walnut trees that have yellowed with autumn like the cottonwoods. They catch sight of a mule deer ahead, as it pauses to look at them before disappearing. A butterfly trails through the air between them, hovering low near their heads, until they're almost out of the grove. On the other side are more open plains, a huge pasture meant for livestock grazing that leads to the hills. They stop the horses with the trees at their backs and look out at the land.

Perched on a log somewhere in the middle of the pasture is a row of lidless jars and beer cans.

"Did you bring it?" Montgomery says, eyeing the log.

Sam reaches into his jacket and pulls his sidearm from the holster on his belt. The Yavapai County Sheriff's Department doesn't issue weapons to their deputies but requires them to carry their own at all times while on duty. Sam never owned a gun in California except the one Lassen County gave him. Holding this one in his hand now, he stills finds it weird that it's his, not something he can leave behind with the job. It was easy enough to get— firearm possession laws in Arizona are laughable— and he figures it would be easy enough to sell it if he wanted to.

Montgomery looks over at him, sees the gun in Sam's hand, and swings off his horse. He walks several yards ahead and stops, feet planted in a wide stance and the wispy grass brushing below his knees.

Sam re-holsters his gun and has an awkward time of dismounting Cavendish, who is unbelievably patient for an animal bearing the weight of a grown man. Once he's on the ground, he's surprised to feel that his ass and thighs hurt like he's been in the gym for a couple hours. He walks up to Montgomery's side and waits for instructions.

Montgomery brandishes his own weapon, the gun he used to shoot Ed Decker in the Dog Bowl Diner. He shows it to Sam. The frame is a clean stainless steel, and the grip is a rich, nutty brown wood. It's obvious that Montgomery takes good care of it.

"Good 'ol Smith and Wesson, .45 ACP, eight rounds in the mag and one in the chamber," he says. "You?"

Sam holds out his gun in his right palm. It's a Ruger LCRX .38 Special, a small black revolver loaded with hollow point bullets powerful enough to kill a man at point blank range with one shot. It's the lightest gun Sam's ever handled and easy to conceal. Maybe a revolver's a little old-fashioned, and maybe a man should carry something bigger, heavier, flashier. But Sam liked the Ruger as soon as he picked it up in the gun store.

Montgomery nods at the weapon. "All right."

He steps forward a couple paces past Sam, squares his stance and his shoulders, and aims his pistol with both hands wrapped around the grip. He stands there for a moment, body relaxed, just pointing the gun.

He shoots left to right, hitting only the beer cans, pausing between each gunshot and explosion of aluminum. Birds rush out of the trees behind them, and the noise echoes through the otherwise quiet landscape.

Montgomery stops halfway across the log and turns around to face Sam. "You been to ranges, haven't you?"

"Yeah, of course," Sam says. A cop has to know how to shoot properly and be able to hit a target, if he's going to carry a weapon, and he's obligated to carry one. He just never made a hobby of shooting. And in Lassen County, California, population 32,136, he only ever had to draw his weapon maybe two or three times. He's never fired it on the job.

"You know your way around that six-shooter?"

"Five, actually. I've put... maybe fifty rounds through it?"

Montgomery nods and gestures at the targets with his hand. "Have at it, Deputy."

Sam moves past him until he's within range of the targets and aims at the first jar on the left, mimicking Montgomery by using both hands to grip the revolver. He looks at the jar through the gun sight, tries to clear his mind, and pulls the trigger.

He almost misses the jar, hitting it near the mouth in its right shoulder and breaking it into several pieces. He moves his eyes and the gun to the next jar, thumbs the hammer down, and shoots. He hits the center of the jar, and it bursts, pieces flying in all directions and the sound of the glass shattering rattling through the pasture.

He misses the next jar, then hits it on his second try. He burns with embarrassment, feeling Montgomery watching him, but moves on without comment. He hits the next two jars on his first attempts and stops where Montgomery did, leaving the other half of the target line-up.

Montgomery steps up alongside him on Sam's right. He doesn't say anything, just looks at the log with his hands on his hips. The sun's higher in the sky now, the landscape brighter and the air a little bit warmer.

"You shoot out here a lot?" Sam says.

"Not a lot," says Montgomery. "Usually don't have the time when I'm working and I don't want to scare the cows too much. Or the horses."

He pulls his pistol from the holster again and shoots his next beer can one-handed. He uses his left, Sam notices.

"Bill and I been shootin' a time or two. Rifles."

"You hunt?" says Sam.

"Only when somebody like him asks me to," Montgomery says, as he lifts his cigarette to his mouth again. "I don't enjoy doing harm to nature. I like a good steak as much as the next guy, but that don't mean I want to butcher the cow."

He shoots the next jar and the next, body loose and almost lazy. Sunlight curls up in the brim of his hat like a cat content to sleep there, and the plains grass rustles in the breeze around his legs. He lowers his gun and just stares at the remaining targets, waiting for Sam to take his turn.

Sam moves to Montgomery's right and aims for the first remaining can. Shards of glass left on the log flash when they catch the light, and the can follows suit, winking at him before he blows it to hell.

# CHAPTER FOUR

It takes some digging, but Montgomery finds her: Donna Rey, the blonde with the big breasts. She has a little house in Dewey, east of the 69. A shoebox house, painted a pastel blue with a dark shingled roof and white trim. She's single and lives alone with her two dogs. He knocks on her door late one Wednesday afternoon, about a week and a half after riding with Sam, and when she answers, she's barefoot in a pair of cut-off denim shorts and a white blouse. She has her hair up in a messy, just-rolled-out-of-bed style, and it looks soft, pieces of it hanging around her face. She reminds him of the pinup models he'd see in his dad's skin magazines from the 70s, stashed away in an old portable cooler in the garage. Innocent baby blue eyes and peachy cheeks. She's wearing a lot of black mascara. He can tell she's in her mid- to late thirties, but she looks younger.

"Can I help you?" she says.

"Donna?"

"Yeah?"

"I need to talk to you about Joel Troutman."

She gets that caught look on her face. "Come on in."

Montgomery follows her inside, holding his hat in both hands and stepping on the carpet like he doesn't want to disturb the house. He can see the dogs watching him from the other side of the sliding glass door leading into the backyard. They don't bark. They just look at him.

Donna goes into the kitchen and takes a couple glasses from the cupboard. "You want something to drink? Water, lemonade, iced tea?"

"Iced tea'll be fine," he says, just to oblige her hospitality.

She pours it into both glasses, and he sits at the kitchen counter opposite her, his back to the living room.

"Did he tell you about me?" she says.

"No," says Montgomery. "Somebody at Billy Jack's told me about you and Joel. I had to find you on my own."

She ducks her head like she's embarrassed that anybody remembers seeing her and Troutman in public together.

"Let's not give each other the run-around, all right? You know he's been missing since he held-up that diner in Prescott, don't you? I want to know where he might be."

"Why?" she says, blue eyes rolling up to meet his, voice breathy and low.

"His wife's looking for him," Montgomery says.

"Oh, my God," says Donna. "Does she know about me?"

He pauses for effect, blinking his languorous eyes at her. "No. I don't have any reason to tell her about you. She asked me to help her find him before the cops do, so that's what I'm doing."

Donna raises her eyes to the ceiling, as if thanking God. She looks cherubic when she does, blonde hair like a halo.

Montgomery wonders why she's the secretive

type mistress instead of the vindictive exhibitionist kind. Does she love Joel Troutman? Enough to want to make his life easy at her own expense? Can she love him that much and still give him up to a stranger?

"Do they know for sure it was him?" she says, hope and dread blended in her eyes. "I've been going kinda crazy ever since he disappeared. I haven't been able to ask anyone about him, and he hasn't called or anything."

"As far as I know, they're sure," Montgomery says. "They didn't see his face or nothing, but he went missing the day of the robbery. No reason to make yourself scarce if you're innocent."

She wilts, gaze falling to the countertop. She's always wanted to believe that Troutman is better than he is, Montgomery can tell.

He sips his tea and lets the truth sink in.

"What's his wife going to do?" Donna says. "If he comes back? Is she going to leave with him?"

Montgomery watches her, pausing before he answers. "I don't know. I think right now, she's just a panicked woman who wants to talk to her husband."

Donna closes her eyes and presses the heels of her hands to her forehead, fingertips against her scalp. She breathes. "I can't believe this is happening. I can't believe he would do something like that. Why would he do something like that? Does he really need the money that bad? He never told me..."

Montgomery hunches over, elbows on the counter, curling his hand around his glass. "You know where he might be, Donna?"

She glances at him. Snags her bottom lip in her teeth. She's trying to decide whether helping him would be protection or betrayal.

Montgomery looks into her eyes and thinks of Sam. "If he's going to get out of this, he needs somebody on his side. We can't help him if he's in the wind."

She folds her hands around the base of her glass and looks into her iced tea. They're feminine hands, fingertips narrow and pointed, nails long and manicured.

Montgomery stares at her and wonders, where did she think her relationship with Troutman was headed? What's this woman's story? What makes her the woman who became Troutman's mistress?

"There's this place," she says. "An old trailer where we would meet to be together. I've wanted to go so many times since he left, see if he might be there, but—I'm afraid." She almost laughs, breaking into a toothy smile. "I don't know why. Maybe I'm afraid he won't be there, you know? That he's really gone."

Montgomery sets his glass down and leans forward, arm underneath him on the counter. "Where?"

*~*~*

She's on top of him, knees in the mattress, back arched and eyes closed with her face tipped up to the ceiling. Her tits jiggle and her sighs fill the room over the sound of the creaking bed springs. Sam watches her, sweat broken across his brow, until he's so close that it hurts. He keeps one hand on her

47

hip, reaches up and grips the headboard with the other, trying to pump into her faster but her weight limits his movement. She leans forward, plants her palms on his chest, and clenches around him. They come within seconds of each other. She makes an animalistic noise, half groan and half shout, grinding against him, and he squeezes her ass, whimpering with his eyes closed. She collapses onto him, hot and limp, and he keeps thrusting until his body stills itself.

They lie there, motionless, for a while. Catching their breath. Her face is covered in a curtain of blonde hair, and he can smell her shampoo and rose-scented soap on her skin. She rolls off of him and lies in the bed next to him for a few minutes, before getting up and crossing the room to the tall wooden dresser. She retrieves her pack of cigarettes and lighter, lights one up, and lopes back to the other side of the room. Sam watches her. She's tall for a woman, about five nine, with a long back and slender limbs. Narrow hips and wide shoulders, a little bit of muscle in her arms. She has a slim waist but a soft belly. She picks her silk robe off the hook on the back of the door, puts it on, and stretches out in the big, upholstered armchair facing her corner of the bed. The robe is midnight blue with tiny white dots all over it; the hem and the ends of the sleeves are striped with rosebud pink, green and white paisley, and a row of birds with their wings outstretched. She almost looks like an old movie star in it, with the cigarette in her hand.

She smokes in silence until Sam sits up, his back against the pillow and headboard. She watches him, and he avoids her at first, then looks at her. She grins, and he smiles in turn.

"You're good, Deputy," she says. "Better than I expected."

"I don't know," says Sam. "Seems to me you do most of the work."

"I know what I like. But don't sell yourself short." She draws on the cigarette and taps the ash into a metal plate on the floor that he told her to use the first time she came over. "It's about time for the talk, isn't it?"

"What do you mean?"

"I mean, the conversation about keeping this casual. You tell me that you like me, but you aren't ready for anything serious. Reassure me more times than necessary that it's really got nothing to do with me, to make yourself feel better. I accept it gracefully and go home, after agreeing to call you when I want to fuck again."

Sam ducks his head, arms draped over his knees in front of him.

"Except," she says, "that conversation is pointless because I don't want this to be more involved either."

He looks up at her again, surprised.

She smiles, satisfied with herself, and smokes. "Don't get me wrong. You're a great guy, Sam. But I'm happy with my life the way it is. And I had a feeling the moment I met you that you're not exactly desperate for a girlfriend. That's one reason I picked you."

He almost laughs. "Well, it's obvious who the smart one is," he says.

She slouches in the chair, reaching her long legs to touch the corner of the bed with her feet. "Any other single woman in this town would definitely meet your expectations," she says. "You just so happened to run into the exception."

Lauren Baker is nothing like Sam's ex-wife. She reminds him of a lion, with her platinum blonde hair and dark brown eyes and the way she prowls wherever she goes. No matter what she wears, she looks ready to strip it off. She's more sexually aggressive than just about every woman Sam's been with. In her late-thirties, she's never been married nor had kids, which is peculiar for a woman in these parts. A native of Flagstaff, she moved down to Prescott five years ago because she wanted to distance herself from the people she knew. Sam gets the impression that he has no idea who she really is. "Lauren Baker" could be a fake name; it wouldn't surprise him.

Like many of Prescott's residents who aren't retirees, she lives in town rather than outside its limits. She has a college degree in astronomy, spent ten years with the Flagstaff Fire Department after graduation, and now works an administrative customer service job at an auto shop. She drives a salmon pink 1957 Lincoln Premiere, and she likes to drink whiskey straight out of the bottle. Her favorite pastimes include throwing darts in bars, screwing male tourists, and climbing trees. When Sam met her in the summertime, she wore denim shorts on the weekends that barely covered any thigh, paired with expensive red cowboy boots several years old. She has great legs and a great laugh.

They sit in silence for a while, as Lauren smokes in the chair and Sam watches her.

"Am I allowed to ask you a personal question?"

he says.

She gives him a saucy grin. "You're a sheriff's deputy. I think you can interrogate me anytime you want."

"Do you have any close friends here? In town?"

"I think we're getting closer every time we see each other," she says, playful and flirtatious.

He wants an honest answer to his honest question, but he doesn't know how to ask her to drop the sexy act without sounding rude. "I mean, are you close to someone that you aren't having sex with? Someone you can count on, who really knows you and cares about you? Maybe even loves you?"

She holds the cigarette in her fingers and stares at him without any flirty suggestiveness. She takes a drag. "There are people I like, who like me. Most of them are men. Some of them I've been with, and some of them I haven't. It's hard for me to keep other women as friends. They're always worried I'll steal their boyfriend or their husband or the guy they want to be with. Or we just don't have enough in common."

"So, no one close? No best friend?" Sam says.

"No, I guess not," says Lauren. She puffs on her cigarette, her hand elegantly posed. "Why? Are you in the market?"

He smiles, mouth waving only for a second. He looks down at his lap. "Maybe. Maybe I'm just lonely. I've been here four months, and I don't really have any friends. I don't see the other deputies outside of work, and there don't seem to be many guys my age in this town, let alone ones who aren't married with kids."

"I know how you feel. Sort of. Married people

are no fun—and even if they could be, they don't usually want to spend time with someone who reminds them what it was like to be free."

Sam pauses, and she looks at his face.

"What?" she says.

He shakes his head. "I'm divorced, and if I'm any freer than I was married, it doesn't feel like much."

"Do you miss your ex?"

There is no simple answer to that question. Sam thinks of Jen less now than he used to, less than he did when he first moved to Prescott, but sometimes, he does miss her. He suspects that most of it is about not having anybody in his life that he feels bonded to, the way he once did with her. He doesn't regret the split. He wouldn't go back to her even if he could. But when he's home alone at night, watching television, or lying awake in bed, he wishes he could call her—just to hear a familiar voice. It's hard to miss who she was and what they had when they were falling in love, without forgetting that she isn't that woman anymore and he isn't that man and even if they reconciled now, their relationship wouldn't be the one that he remembers when he looks at the only wedding photo he kept.

"No," he says to Lauren. "I guess I don't know how to be single anymore. It's not the same as it was when I was in my 20s."

"Of course not," Lauren says, sitting up and dropping her cigarette butt in the ashtray on the floor. "But hey, you got divorced for a reason, right?"

Sam nods. "Yeah, I did." He runs his hands back through his hair and exhales, resting his elbows on his knees in front of him, the sheet tented around him. He looks at Lauren and debates talking to her about something else that's been on his mind. He decides to take a chance. "You ever been in love?"

She laughs, leaning back in the chair again, her feet on the floor now. "Hell, I don't know. I thought I was a bunch of times in high school and college, but I'm pretty sure that was just me being a horny kid with a big imagination. I've never met anyone I wanted to be with the rest of my life. If I had, I would've married him."

He pauses, before asking his next question. "You ever have feelings for another woman?"

Lauren looks at him like he's joking. "No," she says. "Why? Do you fuck men?"

Sam shakes his head. "I didn't ask about sex. I asked about feelings."

"Well, shit, Sam, feelings usually go hand in hand with sex, don't they? Unless you're talking about some other kind I know nothing about."

He's not sure what he's talking about. He's only ever dated women. He's never wanted to have sex with men, but there have been a couple times in his past where he thought he felt something for a man that wasn't any different than the romantic love he'd felt for ex-girlfriends. His best friend in high school was Brian Dunne. He remembers star gazing with him in a field one night when they were seventeen, after splitting a six pack Brian took from his dad's stash. He looked at Brian's face in the dark and felt the most intense love he'd ever felt. Sam wanted to kiss him.

In college, his closest friend was a guy named Andy Albright. They got drunk together once, right after Melanie Schaefer dumped Andy, and made out with each other in the privacy of Sam's bedroom after returning from the bar, falling asleep in his bed together. Afterward, they pretended like nothing happened, and their friendship survived until graduation.

He's never told anyone about the feelings he had for those friends or the desire for physical intimacy. Not even his ex-wife knew. It used to scare him, and he would do his best to ignore and forget about it, in part to avoid overanalyzing himself. He didn't want to be gay or bisexual, didn't know how he would handle it, didn't want to fool around with men just to prove something. His attraction to women had always been clear, since he was a teenager who couldn't be physically close to a pretty girl without feeling his whole body burn and his groin throb. Making out with Josie Lloyd in the back of his big sister's car drove him crazy with the need for more, and he'd think about her naked, the shape and softness of her breasts, when he lay in bed at night and jacked off. But how he felt about the men he was friends with, what he wanted from them, was always hazy and elusive. It hinged on an emotional closeness that slipped through his fingers every time he tried to grasp it and had all but evaporated the moment he finished college. He didn't know how to even begin to create a close friendship with another man as an adult, so he threw himself into his romances with women instead, hoping that he'd get married one day and never want for anything else.

Since horseback riding on the Barbee ranch, Sam and Montgomery have seen each other a few more times, each meeting lasting for hours. They talk, but whenever Sam tries to think of what he knows about the other man, he doesn't come up with much. The more time they spend together, the more Sam likes him, and he can't explain why. He has to remind himself not to be too eager for Montgomery's attention, which makes him feel like a puppy dog. It doesn't help that he still can't tell if Montgomery likes him back or if he's simply tolerating Sam.

"Hey," Lauren says. She rises out of the chair and steps along the foot of the bed, turning to face Sam. "Do you want me to leave or should I take off this robe again?"

One slender eyebrow is slightly arched and lifted, and she looks like she's holding back a smile.

Sam looks at her and decides that he shouldn't mention Montgomery. "You know," he says. "We're allowed to hang out with our clothes on, even though we aren't dating."

Now she does smile. "I know."

"I don't want you to go."

"Okay."

"Want to see if there's anything on TV?"

"You got any cold beer?"

Sam nods.

She turns around and moves to where she left her clothes strewn on the floor. She drops her robe, her backside to him. Peeks over her shoulder just for a second, eyes coy.

He watches her get dressed.

# CHAPTER FIVE

It's a Friday night at the Fool's Gold Saloon, and Montgomery's drinking. He sits at the bar with his arms on the bar top and shot glasses lining up in front of him. There's a pretty good crowd behind him, typical for the weekend. The saloon's closer to Skull Valley than Prescott is, and there aren't more than a couple places to go in town on the weekends. Like many dive bars and saloons in remote parts of Arizona, Fool's Gold sees plenty of bikers, guys who ride up and down the state when the weather's decent. Half a dozen of them are here tonight, their Harleys outside the saloon front like modern-day horses tied up at the drinking trough. Most nights Montgomery comes, he sees a handful of other ranch hands, usually wearing cowboy hats. Some of them he knows and some of them he only recognizes. They tend to be the youngest ones present, men in their twenties and thirties. The rest are older residents of Skull Valley with the kind of personality that sends them here instead of some Downtown Prescott bar or restaurant with a grade or two more class.

After Donna Rey gave him directions to the mobile home she and Joel Troutman used for sex, Montgomery drove east past Dewey-Humboldt proper into the boonies and located the old Airstream. It's sitting alone past a smattering of trees, up a winding dirt road, invisible from Highway

169. Nobody could just stumble upon it by accident or find it without precise directions. Montgomery only got close enough to see it without being seen. Joel Troutman's blue pick-up was parked outside the mobile home, and he didn't want to risk getting caught.

He's been sitting on the information ever since, trying to pick his next move. If he wants to do the right thing, he'll give up Joel Troutman to the Sheriff's Department—but Montgomery might like doing the wrong thing. He might like killing the asshole and keeping the money, because that's as much justice as the alternative would be. Troutman's not just a man who robbed a diner full of good people, he's a cheating husband who was always going to break his lover's heart as much as his wife's. Death might be too harsh a punishment for him, but nobody can argue with the fact that the world would be better off without Troutman in it. Montgomery's been thinking about Troutman's wife. He's been thinking about Donna Rey, with her angelic blonde hair and blue eyes. He's been thinking about that night in the diner, killing Ed Decker.

And that's not all Montgomery's chewing on. He's thinking about Deputy Sam Roswell. He doesn't let on, but he likes Sam. Likes him too much too soon and doesn't know what the hell to do about that. Montgomery hasn't been close to anyone in a long time. Not since he was married. He gave up on it, maybe swore off it without realizing. He got comfortable being alone, a man with no attachments. Spending time with Sam is starting to feel like getting kicked in a bruised place, and

Montgomery is too grown and too smart to believe that, after a long history of heartbreak, he could be in for something different this time.

He tells the bartender he's coming back, then goes to the men's room. He steps outside through the back door to smoke a cigarette, and the cold air feels good on his face after sitting inside for a couple hours. He enjoys the silence. The music playing inside sounds muffled through the walls, and there isn't even the sound of cars passing by the saloon on Iron Springs Road. There's nothing else in between Skull Valley and Prescott except this place, the lights in the windows and the neon sign strange and unexpected as UFO orbs in the blackness. Fool's Gold has been open since the 70s, when Skull Valley was even smaller than it is now and most of Prescott's residents and tourists were part of the mining boom. The saloon used to be a roadhouse but closed its boarding rooms in the 90s, once Prescott got itself a few more hotels.

Montgomery looks at the stars in the sky and tries not to think about Sam. He looks at them and remembers the night sky in South Texas, the thick comforter from his bed wrapped around his favorite woman and his arms around her, too, the two of them standing on the back porch because he tried not to smoke inside and she'd followed him out.

"Fuck it," he says under his breath and drops his cigarette butt on the ground.

He walks around the side of the saloon to the pay phone still installed there, slides a few quarters into the slot, and dials one of the few numbers he has memorized. Listens to the phone ring, half-hoping nobody picks up.

"Hello?" she says.

He almost closes his eyes, doesn't quite smile, sags against the wall with the phone pressed to his ear. That voice hasn't changed at all since the last time he heard it.

"Hello?" she says again.

"Al," Montgomery says. "It's your ex-husband."

"Oh, my God. Mud Pie?"

He grins at the old nickname. "Yeah, it's me. Did I wake you up? I know it's not a good idea calling this time of night, but I was thinking about you and..."

"It's all right," she says. "Daniel ain't here, I've got the house to myself for the weekend. He's on a trip with his brother..."

So she's still with him—Daniel Lynch, the man she met not long after the divorce was finalized. Montgomery saw him once, when he showed up unannounced at the house to drop off the dog for Al to keep. It was just before he left Texas six years ago. The two men eyed each other, wary and tense, over her shoulder. They didn't speak to each other directly, like they both wanted to pretend the other wasn't there.

"Where are you?" Annalee says.

"At a bar," says Montgomery. "Just north of Skull Valley, Arizona, where I live."

"Arizona still. I thought you must've been in California by now. Or Alaska."

"What the hell would I do in Alaska?"

She laughs. "I don't know, kill bears."

Montgomery smiles, his heart in that bittersweet twist she always works it into.

"Are you all right?" she says.

"Yeah. I'm fine. You?"

"I'm good. Everything's real good here."

"I'm glad," Montgomery says, and he is. He's never wanted anything for her but peace and happiness.

"There must be some reason you're callin'," she says, after a pause.

He's quiet as he decides how to ask it. "I need you to answer a question for me, and I need you to be honest."

"You know I always am."

He does. They never lied to each other, except when he had to. "Was I a good friend?" he says. "I mean, aside from us being married and all."

"Montgomery. You were my best friend. The best I've ever had." She says it like she can't believe he doesn't know, a little bit breathless. "I don't think I'll ever have another friend as good as you."

He shuts his eyes and hangs his head, back against the cold wall of the saloon and the sole of his right boot flat on it, too. Now, he aches—for her and what they had.

Montgomery was twenty-three years old when he met Annalee Ford at a Fourth of July party outside Luckenbach, Texas. She smiled with blinding white teeth, laughed and danced all night, and he watched her unnoticed in the crowd, the only young man who didn't try to flirt with her. She introduced herself to him, looking at him with something in her eyes he still can't define, and to this day, he doesn't know how or why she saw him at all.

They were friends for three years before she kissed him one night like she'd been waiting a long time to do it. He never tried making a move on her because he didn't want to. He loved her more than all his other friends, but it didn't occur to him to ask her on a date because romance wasn't something he wanted or felt. Neither was sex. He'd done it with a few girls in high school and college, but he never liked it. Didn't even think about it unless somebody else brought it up.

When Annalee kissed him, he liked the intimacy, but it didn't change how he felt about her. He agreed to date her because he did love her and wanted to be the most important person in her life, even if he wasn't in love with her. He had sex with her because he knew she wanted it, knew he was supposed to, and those first few years, he didn't mind so much. He asked her to marry him because he'd always figured he would get married—didn't want to be alone his whole life and what else was there?—and if there was any woman in the world he could like more than Al, he couldn't imagine who she might be.

But his tolerance for sex started to wane a couple years into the marriage and even before he quit initiating altogether, she could tell something was off. She wasn't a woman who needed a lot of romance, and Montgomery was pretty good about doing sweet things for her. But she could feel the absence of whatever romantic, erotic energy she was used to receiving from her lovers. That was the one thing he couldn't fake. It didn't help that eventually she had to ask her husband, a man in his late twenties and early thirties, for sex if she had any hope of getting laid on a regular basis. At some point, he realized that he couldn't be the man she needed and couldn't live with himself if he tried keeping her anyway.

"You know, I've thought about it a million times," she says. "Asked myself if I should've tried harder, if I should've given it more time, if there was something else we could've done, some way we could've stayed together. And you know what I think?"

He doesn't answer.

"Maybe we should've stayed friends all along. Maybe marrying you was a mistake. My mistake. And if we hadn't done it, you'd still be here. I'd still have you in my life."

He hears the regret, longing, and sadness in her voice, and it wrenches him. He quit trying to figure out how things could've gone differently between them a long time ago. Hearing her say that she shouldn't have married him hurts more than he could describe, but he can't argue with it. In the end, they arrived at the decision to end their marriage together. She didn't need convincing, and he didn't put up a fight.

"I don't mean that I'd take it back," Al says. "I'm just sorry that I hurt you and I'm sorry that I drove you away."

"You didn't," says Montgomery. "You didn't do anything wrong, Al. I made my choices. I wasn't honest with you, and I should've been. Should've been honest with myself."

They're quiet for a minute, listening to each other's silence. Montgomery scrubs the back of his head, looks toward the front of the saloon and doesn't see anything move.

"You know I want you to be happy, right?" she says. "God, I think about you all the time. I think, somebody better come along and love him better than I could."

He smiles, but his chest still feels stuck full of broken glass.

"That why you called?"

"Something like that," he says. "I don't want another wife, Al."

She sniffs and sounds a little more light-hearted. "Well, that's all right. It's not about gettin' married, Mud Pie. It's about having somebody that makes you happy."

Montgomery considers telling her about Sam, only for a moment, then decides it's too soon. He checks his watch. "Guess I better get going. You probably want to go to bed."

She pauses, then says, "You ever get sick of everyplace else, you come on home, okay?"

"Yeah," he says, voice raspy.

It's the kind of thing they both know probably won't ever happen.

"Montgomery," she says.

"Yeah, Al."

"I miss you."

He misses her. Every day. Every time he looks at the night sky, when he sees a peach pie that she didn't bake, when he falls asleep alone in his bed and when he wakes up without a warm body next to him.

"Take care of yourself," he says, and hangs up before he can find out whether or not either one of them is about to burst into tears.

*~*~*

They're stretched out in the bed of Montgomery's pick-up truck, parked in the middle of a field somewhere in West Skull Valley. The sky looks like they're on the inside of a cotton candy maker, gauzy layers of purples, pinks, and blues swirling around them in the last half hour of dusk. The sun's already disappeared into the mountains, and a few stars show themselves sharp and bright high above the horizon line. The grass is still a yellowed green this late in the fall, but the hackberry trees are bright red, only a few of them dotting the plains.

"You any closer to finding Troutman?" Montgomery asks, looking into the distance behind the truck.

"Not that I know of," says Sam. "I'm not really supposed to be involved in hunting him down, on account of I was at the diner that night, but the sheriff and the other deputies keep me informed."

"They afraid you'll kill him if you get the chance?"

Montgomery smiles as he says it, like the idea's ridiculous. Sam doesn't know if he should feel offended or flattered.

"It's protocol," he says.

"Are you abiding by it on your own time?"

Sam glances at him. "I may have been out to Dewey a time or two since the robbery."

"You talk to his wife?" Montgomery says.

Sam nods. Willa Rae Troutman is a blue-eyed brunette in her late twenties with the kind of face that blends in when she's at the grocery store with no makeup on but could win her a modeling career if anybody ever saw her outside Dewey, Arizona.

She had her and Joel's baby on her hip when Sam knocked on her door, the boy no older than two with silky hair and pouty lips. She works part-time at Starbucks and ever since Joel disappeared after the robbery, she's been trying to pick up extra hours and limit how much money she takes out of the Troutman joint checking account, in case he never makes it back. She tried to put on a brave face, talking to Sam, but eventually, she broke down apologizing for what Joel did. Said she didn't know what she was going to do.

"I've been mulling it over," Sam says, looking out the back of the truck bed, past his shoes. "And I don't think Troutman's a bad guy. I think he's somebody who made a bad decision that went sideways on him, and he doesn't know how to get out of the hole."

"And again, I'm telling you that plenty of people got money troubles, but most of 'em don't go holdin' up businesses at gunpoint, truckin' with would-be killers."

"Who's to say Troutman ever would've robbed anyone, without Ed Decker involved? If you ask me, Decker was the mastermind. Without him, Troutman wouldn't have had the stones to rob the diner. And if you remember, he was the one who wanted to take the money and go without hurting anybody. Decker was the dangerous one. That's why he's dead."

Montgomery doesn't reply, and they lapse into silence again. They can hear pinyon jays singing in the distance. Eventually, Montgomery lights up a cigarette.

"Can I ask you a personal question?" Sam says.

Montgomery glances at him. "Yeah."

"Why don't you have any other friends around here?"

"Who says I don't?"

Sam looks at him. "Do you?"

Montgomery pauses. "No."

"Why not?"

Montgomery blows a stream of smoke out his mouth and taps his cigarette over the side of the truck bed. "I told you, people wear on me. It's enough to work with them all day, five days a week, and that's when talk's at a minimum."

Sam thinks about it, then says, "Am I wearing on you yet?"

Montgomery doesn't look at him, his eyes fixed on a tree some distance from the truck. "No," he says.

Sam holds back a smile. "You got any dinner plans?"

"Nope."

"I could go for a cheeseburger and a cold beer."

Montgomery smokes, the brim of his hat casting a shadow over his face. "I could take you to the Kirkland Steakhouse. But it's south of here, about ten minutes if you drive slower than I do."

Sam grins this time. "How long does it take you?"

"From the town center, probably five."

"That's not bad."

Montgomery collapses onto his back, holding his cigarette above him against the side of the truck. He closes his eyes, then opens them again and looks up. It's starting to get dark now, the pinks and purples gone. "Does the rest of the sheriff's department know you've been talking to me?" he says.

"No," says Sam. "Why?"

"No reason."

Montgomery lies there for a minute, then sticks his cigarette in his mouth and swings over the side of the truck. He has to round the back to the driver's door, and when he reaches the tail end, Sam says,

"What are you going to do when you get tired of Skull Valley?"

Montgomery freezes, looking at him with the cigarette in his lips and the wings of his cowboy hat touching the sky. "Hell, I don't know. Why do you ask so many questions? Get outta there, unless you want to ride in the back all the way down."

Sam climbs out of the truck bed and gets into the cab.

It's dark by the time they reach the highway.

# CHAPTER SIX

He's in the diner again, a gun pointed at his chest, the flat surfaces of the room glaring white and the chrome edges glinting in his peripheral vision. This time, it's Joel Troutman aiming at him and he's got a rifle, not a handgun. He isn't wearing a sock mask; Sam's looking right at him, at his face and his eyes clear as the Arizona sky without a cloud in sight.

"You can go," Sam tells him, his hands up in front of him. "I'm not going to chase you."

Troutman watches him with a strange lack of urgency. There's no bag of money, just him and his hunting rifle, the end of the barrel close enough that Sam could grab it if he wanted. He's no expert on firearms, but he knows that if Troutman shoots him with that thing at point blank range, it's over.

"I won't come after you, I promise. You can walk out of here, get in your vehicle, and leave town. All right?"

"I don't know about that, Deputy," another man says.

Sam immediately recognizes the voice.

Montgomery's standing off to his right, in the aisle between booths adjacent to Sam, just where he was the first night they met. But he's not armed now. He's just standing there looking at Troutman, his face and body nonchalant but his gray eyes sharp like a pair of arrowheads.

Troutman swings his gun away from Sam in a sweeping arc, aiming for Montgomery.

"Don't!" Sam says.

Troutman pulls the trigger. The force of the blast knocks Montgomery to the floor and sends him skidding across a couple feet of black and white linoleum tile. He lies motionless, his limbs catching up with the rest of his body as they sway and collapse.

Troutman turns and runs, the bell on the door jingling as he disappears into the night.

Sam slides to his knees at Montgomery's side, mouth hanging open as he looks at the other man.

Montgomery's eyes are open but blank, fixed on the ceiling. There's a gaping hole in his chest, his shirt in tatters, dark blood splattered all over him and beginning to pool on the floor. Sam doesn't know what to do.

"Montgomery?" he says, voice small. "Montgomery?"

He doesn't get an answer.

Sam's hands hover and move in the air, stretched out but unsure where to touch the body. Perhaps unwilling, like if he doesn't make contact, the mirage will dissolve and Montgomery will walk out of the restroom alive and well. But he blinks and the image doesn't change. The bottom starts to drop out of his stomach, and his eyes well as his hands land on Montgomery's face. The cheeks are still warm, skin tan from working in the sun, stubble like sandpaper against Sam's palms. His thumbs swipe back and forth like windshield wipers over Montgomery's face, and he picks up the heavy head off the floor just a little. The eyes don't track, vacant.

A pair of tears rolls down Sam's face. He sits with Montgomery's head in his lap to wait for the sirens and the lights, hands never leaving the false warmth of the face. The smoke has cleared, but the air still smells like it's burning.

Sam sucks in a breath as he wakes up, alone in his bedroom. The bluish light of early morning filters through the window, leaving most of the room in soft darkness. He looks at the digital clock on his night table and finds he still has thirty minutes before the alarm goes off. He takes a deep breath and closes his eyes, then opens them again on the ceiling. The fear from his dream is already evaporating, replaced with relief, but the image of Montgomery dead stays vivid in his mind.

An hour and a half later, he's stepping into Prescott's Lone Spur Cafe dressed in his uniform. He scans the room until he finds the back of a man's head poking up from a booth, shoulder length black hair tied in a ponytail at the nape of his neck. He beelines for the man and slides into the empty seat opposite him.

"Morning, Jethro," Sam says.

"Good morning, Deputy Roswell," says Jethro, looking down into his coffee. He lifts the white mug to his lips and his dark eyes rise with it, meeting Sam's gaze as he drinks.

Jethro Beauty is a Yavapai Indian. The Yavapai people are split amongst three different reservations in Arizona, one of them right next to Prescott on a mere fourteen hundred acres of land. The Yavapai-Prescott tribe is fewer than two hundred people, most of whom work for the tribe's two casinos, hotel, business park, and the big shopping center leased to white companies serving the town of Prescott. Beauty is chief of the tribal police force, which has only seven other officers, and owns a smoke shop in the Frontier Village shopping center. He and his wife have a few acres of the rez all to themselves. She keeps chickens, and they own a pair of dogs. Their son, an only child, lives in Portland, Oregon. Jethro's first cousin Arthur Whipple is the chief of their tribe.

The lieutenant of North Area Command, Sam's supervising officer at the station in Prescott, introduced Sam to Jethro Beauty as necessary procedure, during Sam's first week on the force. On account of Sam being a new resident of the area and completely unfamiliar with the land and the boundaries separating Yavapai jurisdiction from the sheriff's, Beauty took him on a tour of the rez. They've been meeting once a week for breakfast or lunch ever since—though Sam still isn't sure if they're friends or just two men in the same profession sharing meals.

Sam pulls one of the menus tucked against the wall of the booth behind the chrome napkin dispenser and begins to skim it, as Jethro sits across from him with one hand still curled around the handle of his mug and stares at Sam. Their waitress stops by to fill Sam's water glass and asks him what else he wants to drink. He orders coffee. She comes back a minute later with another white mug. Sam adds creamer, looking at Jethro again.

"Something on your mind?" Jethro says, his voice deep and gravelly.

Sam doesn't answer at first, lifting his mug to his

lips and blowing on the coffee before taking a test sip. It's still too hot and he sets the mug down again. "Do you believe in prophetic dreams?" he says.

"Depends on who's dreaming."

Sam pauses again and scans down one column of his menu.

Even this early on a Tuesday, the Lone Spur Cafe is almost full, smells of bacon, sausage, and maple syrup in the air. It's a small restaurant in the heart of Downtown, popular with locals and tourists for its atmosphere as much as its food. The walls are decorated with antique metal spurs and cowboy tools used in the Old West, horseshoes, mining pans, framed paintings of cowboys on horseback, a few mounted rifles, a glass case showcasing sheriff stars, a real bear skin, an antelope head, and a stag skull. Deer antler chandeliers hang over the booths, and in the cafe foyer, a buffalo head mounted on the wall greets customers, wearing a white cowboy hat. Wooden wagon wheels and donated cowboy boots sit atop the separating wall between the foyer and dining room. In one section of the cafe, dozens of real cowboy spurs, metal stirrups, and other parts hang from the wooden rafters above a row of booths. The place reminds Sam of Montgomery now.

"You got any thoughts on friendship, Jethro?" Sam says.

Jethro continues to look at him with an inscrutable expression. He blinks, drinks his coffee, and doesn't speak for a minute or two.

Sam decides what he wants to eat, as he waits for a response.

"It is a broad subject," Jethro says. He thinks some more. "The happiest men I've known either had a good wife or at least one good friend. It is rare to have both, common to have neither. I think one is much harder to find than the other."

"Which one?" says Sam.

"Which do you think?"

The waitress returns to take the men's orders. Jethro always has the same thing when Sam meets him here for breakfast: Joe's Special. Today, Sam wants two eggs over easy, hash browns, and a biscuit with butter, no gravy.

"You ever have a good friend?" Sam asks, sipping coffee from his mug.

Jethro glances at him, then looks past Sam's right shoulder toward the back of the cafe. "I have had a few," he says. "My brother, James. My cousin, the chief. Outside of my family, Peter Hazelwood was the best friend I ever had. Fellow Yavapai. We met when we were boys."

Sam's never heard of the man, and he would've by now, if Peter Hazelwood was still a resident of the area. "What happened to him?"

"Vietnam." Jethro lifts his mug to his lips and takes a drink. His face, his eyes, and his voice don't give anything away, but the word hanging between him and Sam unexplained is enough to make it clear that forty odd years hasn't cured the pain of Jethro's loss. He's in his mid-sixties now, which would've made him and his friend young men in their early twenties during the tail end of the war. Sam has a feeling that Jethro can still remember Peter's face with perfect clarity. He's almost sorry he asked.

"And you, Deputy Roswell? Have you had better luck with friendship than marriage?"

Sam half shakes his head and shrugs his shoulders a little.

Jethro leans back into his cushioned seat, pose more relaxed. "You're still young," he says. "You have time."

"I don't think time has much to do with it," Sam says. "Seems like it's mostly about luck."

"You have a lot of time to get lucky."

Sam doesn't quite smile and looks down into his coffee. He wonders what Jethro would think of Montgomery. He tries to picture the two men meeting, and he gets the sense that they would like each other in a mutually silent and unenthusiastic way.

"You left no one behind in California worth counting?" says Jethro, looking at Sam now. It's the kind of question that he already knows the answer to but he asks it out of courtesy to the other person.

"If there was someone there worth sticking around for, I would've stayed," Sam says.

Jethro nods.

Sam's thought about tracking down the best friends of his youth, since moving to Prescott, but trying to revive old relationships over long distance doesn't feel like the solution he's looking for. He's been spending more time with Montgomery, and he's hoping that the aloof and enigmatic cowboy is the man he needs. But he can't be sure yet. He's still not convinced that Montgomery wants to be friends with him. It could just be that he's politely indulging Sam.

The waitress serves Sam and Jethro their food,

and they eat in silence for a while.

"The man wanted for robbing the Dog Bowl Diner is still at large," Jethro says, moving food around on his plate with his fork.

"Yes," says Sam.

"Is the Sheriff's Department still actively pursuing him?"

"As far as I know."

Jethro is quiet.

"What?" Sam says.

"Enough time has passed that if you haven't found him, you probably never will."

It's true, so Sam doesn't argue.

He's thought plenty about Joel Troutman in the weeks since the hold-up, usually when he's driving or when he looks out his kitchen window at the mountains in the distance or when he sees Montgomery. Every time he's watched the local news since the hold-up, he's seen Troutman's photo displayed with the Yavapai County Sherriff's phone number, the anchor advising anyone with information on the suspect to call and leave a tip. He hears the locals in town gossiping about Troutman, the robbery, and Ed Decker's death no less now than he did the first week after the incident, and even at work, the other deputies have the same conversations about the case over and over because it's the most exciting thing that's happened in the county in recent memory. He's made multiple visits to Dewey-Humboldt, and he sees the wanted flyers still posted in the gas stations, bars, and store windows when he's down there. The Sheriff's Department considered paying for a billboard along the highway leading into

Dewey-Humboldt, but the cost was outside their budget.

"Did you get a wanted poster?" Sam asks. "With Troutman's picture?"

Jethro glances up at him from his plate. "Yes," he says.

"Do me a favor and keep your ear to the ground, especially when you're off the rez?"

"No need to ask."

They finish their food and their coffee, pay their tabs, and go their separate ways.

*~*~*

Montgomery drives Sam out to one of his favorite spots on the Barbee Ranch, in the cooling dusk of a Saturday night. They lie down in the grass with an ice cold six pack between them, pulled from the portable cooler in the truck bed, and watch as the smear of fiery orange light slowly shrinks into the mountains on the horizon and the stars begin to peep out of the darkening lavender sky. It's getting colder at night now, and soon they won't want to stay outside unless they have to. They're both silent until they've finished drinking their first beers, looking at the landscape together and listening to the birds and the insects and the slightest breeze rustling the plants.

Montgomery cracks open his second beer and says, "So if Joel Troutman ever got found and arrested, what would ya'll charge him with?"

Sam thinks about it, staring at the mountain range silhouetted against the sky now a dark indigo softened in the deepening darkness. "Aggravated assault and armed robbery, for sure. If they really wanted to go after him, they might try tacking on accessory to attempted murder of a police officer, but I doubt a prosecutor could sell that to a jury, when a bunch of witnesses can testify to the fact that he never threatened my welfare directly and tried to convince Decker to leave me alone."

"How much time would he do for the assault and robbery charges?"

Sam blows air through his nose and says, "Hard to say. It depends on the judge. Could be less than five, could be ten or more."

"The bottom line being, that no matter what, his wife's shit out of luck. Bet you there was less than five hundred dollars in that sack Troutman made off with."

Montgomery takes a drink, and Sam doesn't reply.

"Anybody in the Sheriff's Department consider the possibility that she might just run off with him?" Montgomery asks, after a pause.

Sam glances at him. "I don't think she would. Even if Joel came back for her. They have a toddler. She isn't going to become a fugitive and risk losing her son for Joel and a few hundred bucks."

Montgomery doesn't look convinced. "People do stupid things to get out of a bad spot."

"Yeah," Sam says. "But I'm pretty sure Willa Rae wouldn't do something stupid for so little money and no guarantees. Not to mention, she made it clear to me that she doesn't defend what Joel and Ed did."

Montgomery pauses, sips on his beer, sits up with his knees in front of him and the beer can in the grass between his legs. He lights a cigarette, cupping one hand around the end as he does, then rests his arms on his knees and looks over the land. "You ever meet a truly bad man?" he says. "On the job, I mean. Someone who'd done something that'd make people afraid of him."

Sam breaks a second can of beer out of the plastic rings and snaps it open. "I've met some people who broke the law in minor ways. But I don't know about the kind of person you're describing. We never had any murders in Lassen County, while I was there. Or child abuse. Rape. Even the domestic calls were all pretty tame."

Montgomery quirks a corner of his mouth and takes a drag on his cigarette.

"What?" Sam says, catching the smile.

"Just because you never got any calls about murder, rape, and child abuse doesn't mean they ain't ever happened, Deputy."

The suggestion unsettles Sam. "Rate of crime is always proportional to population. Lassen County is mostly rural with a small population spread out all over. Even in the county seat, where we were headquartered, violent crime has always been low. And there's about eighteen thousand people in Susanville."

"Low and nonexistent are two different things," Montgomery says.

Sam doesn't respond, and they're quiet for a few minutes, drinking.

"Been meaning to ask you," says Montgomery, as he lies back down with the cigarette hanging from his lips. He's got his elbows underneath him. "If you'd had your gun that night in the diner, what do you think you would've done?"

Sam looks at him. He hadn't thought about that hypothetical scenario at all, as strange as that may be. "I don't know. I'm sure I would've pulled my weapon on Decker as soon as he snatched up the kid, but after that, it would've come down to his reaction."

"Think you would've shot him?"

Sam hesitates. "It's within my right as an officer of the law to shoot anyone who threatens my life or someone else's. But it's supposed to be my last resort."

Montgomery looks at him. "It's a yes or no question, Sam."

Sam holds eye contact with him and doesn't answer for several seconds. "If he gave me no choice and I had a clear shot," he says.

Montgomery looks away again. "You sound like you'd regret it even if you couldn't do anything else."

"You think I should enjoy shooting people?"

"Maybe not enjoy it. But you can feel justified."

Sam can't know how he would feel after shooting someone until he does it, but he imagines that a sense of righteousness would not be his, regardless of what his victim did to force his hand.

It's dark now, new stars appearing all over the sky with each passing minute but no moon. There isn't an electrical light anywhere in sight. Montgomery gets up and ambles back to the truck, opens the driver's door and leans in to stick his key in the ignition, turning the truck's electrical system on to power the tail lights and head lights. He comes back and reoccupies his spot on the ground next to Sam, the truck's tail lights glowing red behind them just enough that their faces are visible to each other.

Sam watches Montgomery smoke the cigarette, as he nurses his second beer, and wonders again about Montgomery's ex-wife Annalee. Marriages happen and fail all the time, but the story of Montgomery's marriage is an empty shape in Sam's mind that piques endless curiosity, not least of all because Sam can't imagine Montgomery falling in love with anyone, much less what kind of woman it takes to make it happen.

"I know it's a ways off, but I was wondering what your plans are for Thanksgiving," Sam says. "If you go see family or stay here."

Montgomery shoots him a look. "You think I need someone to take me in?"

"Well, I don't know. That's why I'm asking. Somebody's gotta be on call for the department that day, and I volunteered because I'm the new guy. But I got a dinner invitation from Lauren, and I figured if you want company..."

"Who's Lauren?" Montgomery says, staring at the sky and the black shapes of the mountains.

Sam pauses. "This woman I've been seeing."

Montgomery doesn't respond, his mouth set into a flat line and his face inscrutable.

"Well," Sam says. "We're not really dating, we're just—having sex."

"How long's that been going on?"

"A few months."

"You gettin' serious about her?" Montgomery asks, still looking away from Sam.

"No. Not really. I mean, I like her and all, but I

80

don't want it to be more than what it is. Neither does she."

Montgomery looks over his shoulder at Sam with a skeptical eyebrow. "You sure about that?"

"Yeah," Sam says. "Lauren's not like most women. She's—I don't know how to describe it— she's just different."

Montgomery's quiet for a minute, then says, "She your way of gettin' over your wife?"

Sam looks at him. "She's company. She's someone I can have sex with who doesn't want to be my girlfriend, which is just about the last thing I'm interested in right now."

"Hell, you're fixing to have Thanksgiving dinner with the woman. What are you interested in?"

You, Sam thinks.

"Friends can spend holidays together," he says. "Lauren and I like hanging out once in a while, and she's being nice because she knows I don't have any family here, that's all. She's not even going to cook. I think we're ordering take-out or something."

Montgomery finishes his cigarette without any more protest, sticking the butt in one of his empty beer cans. He doesn't look at Sam, but Sam looks over at him every other minute, trying to detect some emotion in Montgomery's face. There isn't any.

"You ever have a best friend?" Sam says, putting on a casual tone. He's on his third beer now.

"No," says Montgomery.

Something about the way he says it—sounds like it isn't the whole truth.

They lie there in silence until the beer's gone, watching the stars. There's too many of them to count without getting lost. Sam can't even make out any constellations.

When they're both sitting in the truck again, Montgomery pauses after starting the engine and looks across the bench seat at Sam in the dark.

"I know where Joel Troutman is," he says.

# CHAPTER SEVEN

Sam goes to find Troutman's hideout by himself after he gets off work on Monday afternoon, taking his own unmarked car instead of his unit. Montgomery never saw Troutman, only a blue pick-up truck parked outside the camper that looked like the same one Troutman used to flee the scene of the robbery. Sam wants to confirm that it's the right man hiding out, before he brings the information to his lieutenant's attention.

He follows Montgomery's directions scrawled on a piece of paper ripped from a notepad, taking the various paved and unpaved roads snaking north off Highway 169, slowing the car as he begins to pass through an archway of leafless trees and brush. The branches reach up and crowd out the sky, white and pointy, like the skeletons of men who died with their hands up. Sam worries that this is the only access road to wherever Troutman's parked his camper, but he keeps driving because this is what Montgomery's note tells him to do.

A few minutes onto this dirt path, Sam sees another one forking off into the trees on his right, just wide enough for him to take it without the limbs scraping against the car. He decides to follow the path and see if it provides a view of Troutman's hideout without leading directly to it. Not knowing how close he is to the campsite and wanting to be as undetectable as possible, he inches the car along as slow as he can. The trail curves to the left, toward the main drag and wherever it leads. Sam keeps going until the trail thins out to a walking path. He can see the old steel Airstream through the trees; the car's facing the campsite. He kills the engine, figuring it's better not to risk anyone hearing it, and waits.

He can make out the blue pick-up truck that Willa Rae Troutman confirmed her husband drives, the same truck that Sam saw Joel drive off in the night of the robbery. But a lot of people in the quad-city area drive trucks, and plenty of them are blue or Fords or both.

Sam checks his watch and settles in. He doesn't have anywhere to be tonight, but he doesn't plan on staking out the campsite after dark. He's got about an hour before the sun sets, maybe less. He switches his cell phone onto silent mode and tries not to wish that he had someone with him in the car.

Forty-five minutes pass. He starts to resign to the possibility that it could take hours for anyone to come out of the camper, let alone leave, when he sees him. Troutman, no different than he was the night of the robbery except for several days' worth of facial hair, swings the camper door open on creaky hinges and lumbers down the steps in a pair of work boots. He's lighting up a cigarette as he moves, and he stops a few yards away from the Airstream and just stands there a minute, surveying his surroundings. He looks up at the sky, probably figuring that nightfall is due within the hour.

Sam holds his breath as he watches, hoping like hell that his vehicle really is as obscured in the bush as he thought it would be when he picked this spot. Troutman's back is to him. It occurs to Sam that maybe he came out of the camper not to smoke but to investigate the noise of Sam's car getting within spying distance. He has no idea what he'll do if he's found.

But Troutman turns around and goes back into the Airstream without a suspicious look on his face and without pausing to check the lot more closely. He reemerges a minute later wearing a jacket with his keys in hand. He shuts the camper door behind him but doesn't lock it, then gets into his blue pick-up and heads down the dirt path.

Sam waits until the sound of the truck fades out into nothing, then grabs his sidearm off the passenger seat and gets out of the car making as little noise as possible. He leaves his badge behind, clipped to the driver's side visor. He's wearing a hooded sweatshirt over a t-shirt and jeans. If he gets caught, nothing about his appearance will give him away as a sheriff's deputy.

It's silent here, except for his own footsteps scratching at the ground. He follows the walking path around to the back end of the camp site, through the dead trees, and wonders if Troutman lies awake at night in partial disbelief that he ended up here, with nothing to show for his sacrifice of wife, baby, and real bed in a real house, except a sad sack of cash that wouldn't last him two weeks on the road as a fugitive. Maybe the money's gone already—spent on food and gas these weeks he's been hiding, to avoid leaving a trail of credit card charges.

Sam cuts through the trees when he's directly

behind the Airstream, pauses and listens, almost afraid that Troutman's about to return right this second. He wishes there was a back door, a second way in and out, but there isn't. If Troutman comes back too soon, Sam's going to have to punch him and run. He rounds the front end of the camper, tense and hyper-alert, and hurries up the fold out steps to the door, which he shuts behind him.

Inside the camper, there's a double bed built into the rear end from wall to wall, an old refrigerator, a couch only deep enough for a man of average build to lie across it length wise, a four-person table with booth seats, a small kitchen with a sink and combination stove oven, a bathroom, several cabinets, and a storage closet. The floor of the camper is a nutty brown wood, and there are several area rugs. An old TV set is sitting on a small table across from the sofa, pushed up against the side of the refrigerator.

The wastebasket is almost overflowing, and there are dozens of empty beer bottles all over the little kitchen counter. Three empty pizza boxes are stacked on top of the refrigerator. There are a few dirty dishes and utensils in the sink and clean ones left out on the drying pad next to it, the glasses and mugs upside down. Troutman's got a vintage pin-up themed calendar tacked to the wall; Miss October's wearing a witch hat and sitting on a giant pumpkin. Sam wants to turn the page—it's November now— but he needs to go undetected. He searches the cupboards and drawers, the refrigerator and freezer, the dishwasher and the oven but doesn't find anything.

There are bottles of nail polish lining one of the

shelves in the narrow bathroom: the first sign of Donna Rey in the camper. Sam also guesses the teddy bear sitting in the corner of the bed belongs to her, too, probably a gift from Troutman. The bed is unmade, and Troutman's dirty clothes have been left in a heap on the floor. A small, potted cactus with one pink flower sits in the window above the bed. The dresser top is covered in loose change, receipts, buttons, condoms, a few business cards, a photo booth strip featuring Troutman and Donna smiling and kissing, a man's watch, a dirty coffee mug, and movie ticket stubs from a theater in Prescott Valley.

Sam searches the skinny closet for the money and the gun but doesn't find anything except some of Troutman's clothes, a vacuum cleaner, and unused hangers. He checks the dresser drawers with no luck but does find a glass pipe with remnants of smoked grass in the top drawer. A smear of lipstick is still caked onto the underside of the pipe's neck. Jen, his ex-wife, used to smoke weed in college and through most of her twenties. She asked him once if he had any drug experience, maybe assuming that a sheriff's deputy would either have none or lie about it if he did. Sam told her the truth, as always. He'd never tried it, and he didn't care that she had.

When he glances up on impulse, he finds a road map of the United States taped to the ceiling above the bed. He can see Troutman and Donna lying in bed together, looking at the map, dreaming out loud about escaping Dewey-Humboldt, Arizona, and traveling the country—knowing the whole time that they never would. He looks down again and sees a baby blue sleeve peeping out of the bedding that's twisted and bunched up. He pulls on it and sees that it's a long button-down shirt, something that must belong to Donna, either something she slept in or wore after sex just to bum around the camp site. It smells a little bit like perfume, something sweet and floral. Sam wonders for the first time how Troutman feels about her, if he loves this woman who isn't his wife or if she's just uncomplicated fun and good sex. If he believes what Donna claims, Troutman hasn't contacted her since the robbery, but then again, he hasn't reached out to Willa Rae either.

Sam goes back to the front end of the Airstream and plops down on the couch with a sigh. Even if the Sheriff's Department arrests Troutman as a suspect in the diner robbery, they can't charge him for anything without hard evidence tying him to the crime. He never took off his mask, so there's no way to make a positive ID based on looks alone. Everyone who was in the diner heard Troutman's voice that night, but witness memory is often shoddy at best. Sam saw him drive off in the blue pick-up but didn't get the plate number, so that won't be enough on its own. Without the cash in the collection sack that Troutman and Decker brought or the gun that Troutman used in the hold-up, there's nothing concrete that ties him to the robbery. He doesn't have an alibi for that night, and his disappearance since doesn't look good. But getting a prosecution team to press charges against him or a jury to convict based on those two details alone would be more than a long shot. Even the stolen money would be a hard sell in court. If it's all cash, no credit or debit cards, proving that it came from the patrons of the diner that night would be next to impossible. The prosecution would have to track Troutman's bank activity to show a jury that the amount of cash, assuming Sam or someone else finds it all, was never withdrawn from the only account that Troutman's got, and even then, it wouldn't be difficult for him to come up with some explanation about where the money came from. They're going to have to search his emails, his text messages, his call log, to find proof of Troutman and Decker planning the robbery. There was nothing on Decker's end that the sheriff's department found.

Maybe Sam was naive to think that he'd find anything here. Troutman could be keeping the money and the gun in his truck. He could've buried the stuff somewhere, for all anyone knows. Or maybe Montgomery was right and Willa Rae is covering for her husband, lying to the cops, hiding the money for him until he figures out what to do. Maybe it's Donna. Neither woman made Sam suspicious, but that doesn't mean they're being honest.

He gets up off the couch and surveys the Airstream interior one last time, about to walk out defeated. He pauses when he notices the coffee can in the kitchen, tucked behind the coffee maker. He peeks out the window to make sure Troutman isn't coming up the dirt road, then moves into the kitchen. He peels the coffee can lid open and there in the dark grounds is a wad of cash rubber banded together. He smiles to himself a little.

Sam checks his watch, looks over his shoulder at the door, then takes the cash out of the can and counts it. Six hundred and seventy-three dollars. He wraps the rubber band around the stack again and puts it back in the can.

He walks out of the Airstream and goes around to the mouth of the path behind it, in no hurry as he returns to his car. He wonders if Troutman keeps a picture of his son in the truck or in his wallet. There's no trace of the boy here.

# CHAPTER EIGHT

Montgomery's soaking in his stand-alone bath tub on a Saturday evening, smoking a cigarette and thinking about the people he's been close to in his life. All of them gone, moved on from him, now different than who they were when he knew them or maybe just in a different place that he wouldn't fit into. The girls he dated before Al, the first in high school and the others in his late teens and early twenties. He sees their faces, remembers the softness of their skin and their hair and the way they looked at him, their lips sometimes smooth and sometimes dry and chapped in the heat or the cold. The smallness of their hands in his, the way they smelled along the slopes of their necks, their floral print dresses and how they talked at him all the time to fill his silence. There were only three before Al, and each one he hoped would be his companion forever. Each one he let go when they tired of him, wanted something or someone else, or sensed that whatever they were looking for Montgomery didn't have.

He thinks about the men, too: his best friend in high school who joined the Army after graduation and the young man he met on his first ranching job, a wrangler who was a few years older than Montgomery. Bo Davis. They used to go drinking at their favorite bar, The Steering Wheel, a roadside dive along Highway 290. They'd disappear from the world for days, herding and caring for cattle on thousands of acres of land and camping on the trail, just the two of them sometimes. Montgomery didn't want for anything when they were alone together in the wilderness. Bo was the one who took Montgomery to that Fourth of July party where he met Al. Bo was the best man at Montgomery and Al's wedding. He was Montgomery's closest friend besides Al until the day Montgomery left Texas in his rearview mirror, unable to follow the other man because of his long-time girlfriend and son in Luckenbach.

There were other men, too, ranch hands in Texas and New Mexico and southern Arizona. Men he worked with every day for ten or twelve hours straight, men he shared meals with three times a day, shoulder to shoulder at the table. He was never as close to any of them as he was to Bo or his high school best friend, but there was something about their collective presence, their voices around him, the heat of their bodies that made him feel less alone in the world. It was easier when he was young, when they were all young and single and childless. There wasn't anything to stand between them, no reason for him to look at those other men hopelessly. Montgomery hasn't spent any time being friendly with the guys he works with on Barbee's ranch here in Skull Valley; by the time he moved to town, he was tired of trying to believe that someone could be the friend he needed.

He used to think it was Al. And some part of him still wants it to be her, holds the image of her face in secret, a fantasy of returning to her and the two of them being happy together as the best of friends.

But Montgomery's not stupid or naïve. He knows that the woman in his fantasy isn't the real Al, that if it could've worked between them, he wouldn't be here now. Still, he lets himself see her sometimes when he closes his eyes, sees their house with the sun setting the sky on fire behind it, remembers when they were happy.

He's wondered one too many times since he left her in Texas, if he's selfish for wanting somebody to be happy with him, to love him for what he can give and not for what he can pretend. He's never met anybody like him, and maybe that's what it would take for a partnership, a friendship, to work out. Somebody like him. Only problem is he doesn't know where to look and he's not about to advertise his oddities.

Montgomery takes a drag on his shrinking cigarette, blowing the smoke up toward the ceiling as he tips his head back against the lip of the tub. He's only thirty-eight years old, and he's fixing to be alone the rest of his life. He's not sure he likes the sound of that. Not sure that he's cut out for it.

He closes his eyes and lies prone in the tub until the water's lukewarm, almost cold, and his cigarette's an extinguished stub in his fingers. He steps out and dries off, puts on some clean clothes and his caramel brown cowboy boots, grabs his keys from the nail in the wall next to the front door, and heads out.

Half an hour later, he pulls up in front of Sam's house and shifts the truck into park but keeps the engine on a minute. The house is an old two-story not far from Downtown Prescott, on a street of homes that look like something copied from a

Christmas gingerbread tin. The outside is painted a faded grayish blue with white trim, and the roof shingles are dark. He peeks at it through the passenger window, then stares through the windshield as he wonders if going in is a good idea.

He doesn't know what he wants with Sam, now or in general. He's aware that he hasn't shown any degree of enthusiasm about being Sam's friend, that he's only accepted requests made for his company without giving any further indication that he wants to spend time with Sam. It isn't that Montgomery is indifferent. He likes Sam. He's always liked Sam, since that night at the Caged Bird Saloon. He just doesn't want to go getting attached to somebody who's bound to disappoint him again. He doesn't want to pin his wish for a partnership that's not sexual or romantic on a guy who's looking for a wife. If he were smart and realistic, he would tell Sam to quit bothering him and be done with it.

But Montgomery cuts the engine of his truck and gets out, sticking his hands into the pockets of his jacket as he goes up the walkway and the porch steps to Sam's front door. He rings the bell and waits.

Sam looks a little surprised when he opens up. "Hey," he says. "Is everything all right?"

"Yeah," says Montgomery. "This a bad time?"

"No. Not at all. Come in."

Montgomery steps inside and takes his time following Sam to the kitchen, looking around at the foyer and the living room on the right, the staircase that leads to the second floor with its polished, dark wood banister. The living room was probably meant to be divided into two areas, shared with a formal dining room. It stretches from the front of the house to the back, taking up the whole eastern half of the first floor. Montgomery's surprised at how well-decorated and furnished it is for belonging to a man who lives alone. It's nowhere near as bare bones as Montgomery's living room, but there's not a whole lot of excess either.

"Can I get you a beer?" Sam calls from the kitchen.

"Sure," says Montgomery, still lingering between the staircase and the living room entrance. He hears Sam retrieve the beers from the refrigerator and pop off the caps with a bottle opener.

Sam comes back out of the kitchen and holds out one of the bottles to Montgomery, who takes it.

"Looks like you got a pretty good porch," Montgomery says.

"You want to sit out there?" says Sam.

Montgomery nods.

They step outside onto the front porch, both of them wearing a jacket, and settle down in the two rubber fold-up chairs Sam's got there. They look aged, maybe secondhand, and it's strange that Sam put them out here in plain view. They clash with the interior of the house, and Montgomery has to ask.

"They run out of real chairs in Prescott?"

Sam smiles and sips on his beer. "I just haven't gotten around to shopping for some. These I brought over from California."

He doesn't elaborate, but Montgomery doesn't need him to. These chairs are relics from Sam's old life, from his dead marriage, and no wonder they look used. Maybe they used to be a part of Sam and

Jen's porch or their backyard deck. Maybe the couple carted the chairs around with them on trips to the beach or the woods when they went camping. When it came time to split up all their possessions, she might've left the chairs behind, and for whatever reason—maybe sentimentalism—Sam packed them into his U-Haul instead of trashing them.

Montgomery didn't take anything from the house he shared with Al. Just his clothes and shoes, his personal items that had nothing to do with her. He left all the framed photographs of them hanging on the walls, the dog, his pale blue wedding tuxedo. He didn't want her haunting him, but maybe he wanted to haunt her a little.

He and Sam sit in silence for a while, drinking from time to time and looking out at the street and the sky, the stars twinkling above the roofs of the houses, the yellow lights glowing in windows and next to front doors.

"I saw Troutman," Sam says, eyes combing over the houses across the street. "You were right. The Airstream's his."

Montgomery looks at him, then back ahead. "When are you going to bust him?" he says.

"Soon. I haven't told my superior officer yet, but I'm sure as soon as I do, I'll get the green light to pick Troutman up."

"Why haven't you said anything?"

Sam pauses, like maybe he's not sure what the reason is. "He's going to do at least three to five. Even if he gets out sooner on good behavior, I can't see him doing any less than two. And his family—"

When Sam doesn't finish the sentence,

Montgomery says, "You feel sorry for him."

"I feel sorry for his wife. And his kid."

"Yeah, well. He's not doing them any good where he is."

Sam doesn't argue, and they fall silent again.

"You want to stay for dinner?" Sam says, looking over at Montgomery.

"Sure."

They order a pizza and drive into Downtown Prescott to pick it up, stopping at a liquor store on the way back for more beer. Sam throws a salad together, and they eat at the kitchen table, silent for much of the meal as music plays on low volume in the background. Once their plates are clean and the pizza box is empty, they start to talk as they work their way through a dozen cans of local beer, taking turns getting up to pick them out of the freezer.

"Let me ask you something," Montgomery says, holding the fifth beer of his pack. "You got designs on the sheriff seat?"

Sam snorts. "I've been in this county less than six months. I don't know how long I'm staying. Right now, I'm happy just to work."

"What about before? In California?"

Sam pauses. "I don't think I ever thought about it. It's the kind of thing you need a certain amount of experience for, in my opinion, and I was happy being a deputy anyway. Still am."

Montgomery sips on his beer.

After a moment, Sam says, "You ever date anybody here? Since you moved to Skull Valley?"

Montgomery glances at him before dropping his eyes to take another drink. "No."

"Haven't met anyone who interests you?"

"I don't date because I don't want to," Montgomery says.

"You still in love with your ex-wife?"

Montgomery doesn't answer.

"I'm sorry," says Sam. "I didn't mean to—it's none of my business. I'm just feeling the beer."

"It's all right," Montgomery says. He finishes his fifth beer, sets the can aside with the others, and opens his last one.

They're quiet for a minute or two, the music no longer playing on Sam's portable speakers.

"Did you go to college?" Sam asks.

Montgomery shakes his head. "No."

"Why not?"

"Wasn't interested. I wouldn't have had the money for it, anyhow. When I got out of high school, I didn't know exactly what I wanted to do with my life, but I reckoned I wasn't the college type."

"I saw the books in your living room," Sam says. "The first time I came to your house."

"Always did like to read," says Montgomery. "Not having a college degree doesn't make a man stupid, Sam. Or ignorant."

"I know. I just think it's weird that someone smart who likes to read chose physical labor over school."

"You went to college and became a sheriff's deputy. Pretty sure the two don't have anything to do with each other."

Sam bobs his head. "Point taken."

Montgomery pauses. "There's no shame in honest work. If it makes you happy and pays the bills, what more can a man want?"

Sam blinks at him, his expression pensive and maybe a little sorry. "I don't think you have anything to be ashamed of," he says.

The empty beer cans huddle together at the edge of the table. Montgomery lights up a cigarette, sprawled out in his chair with his legs stretched in front of him. Sam watches him with his elbows on the table, one hand tented over the top of his last beer. Smoke starts to cloud the air between them, the smell of the Marlboro filling the kitchen. The house is quiet.

Sam gets up and takes the plates to the sink. He collects the beer cans from the table and dumps them in the recycle bin. Montgomery, a little drunk now, continues to smoke his cigarette without thinking anything at all. Sam comes up behind him, rests his hands on Montgomery's shoulders and squeezes, his grip stronger than Montgomery would've expected. Montgomery only tenses against the touch for an instant, before relaxing into it. Sam starts massaging his shoulders, sweeping his thumbs over the back of his neck. Nobody's touched him like this in years, not since Al.

"This okay?" Sam asks.

Montgomery's already got his eyes closed, but he doesn't miss the faint slur in Sam's voice. "Yeah," he says. "Feels good."

"Let me know if it hurts," says Sam.

"Hurt's how you know it's working," Montgomery says.

Sam rubs his shoulders for several minutes, using both the heels of his palms and his fingers. He loosens a few knots, works on Montgomery's neck and the space between his shoulder blades, doesn't hold back on the pressure. When he finally quits and steps away, Montgomery's flesh is warm and tender from the base of his skull through his shoulders and upper back. Sam's hands are warm too, and tired.

Montgomery opens his eyes and breathes. "Thanks. I needed that."

Sam wipes his hands on his jeans. "You're welcome," he says. "Just ask, if you—if you want me to do it again some time."

Montgomery nods, even though his back's to Sam. "I could use a drink," he says. "A real drink. Don't know about you."

"Yeah."

Sam turns and takes a couple glasses out of one of the cabinets and pulls an almost full bottle of Maker's 46 from the top of the refrigerator. He stands at the table next to Montgomery and pours them both a glass.

"I think we'd be more comfortable in the living room," he says, then heads out of the kitchen with the bottle of whiskey and his drink.

Montgomery gets up after a pause and follows him.

Sam's leaning over the fireplace, tossing in a couple logs from the pile in a metal crate to the left and crumpled sheets of newspaper lying on the coffee table. He lights the kindling and tinder with a utility lighter and waits to see the flames catch before straightening up and trading the lighter for the whiskey on the mantle.

As the firelight begins to brighten, the room becomes even more inviting than it was before. The walls are painted forest green, the floor is a dark caramel wood, and the fireplace is exposed brick. Two matching sofas face each other in the center of the room before the fireplace, with a wooden coffee table in between, all standing on a large shag area rug. An old chocolate leather armchair is positioned to the right of the fireplace. Toward the front of the room, a tall bookcase stands against the wall, part of a different section of the long room arranged near the windows that includes a pair of big easy chairs, a smaller sofa, and another table. The television and a large, round sofa chair are in the back.

"You bring all this from California?" Montgomery asks without thinking.

Sam looks over his shoulder at him. "No," he says. "Some of it I ordered from a catalog. Some of it's from Phoenix. Took me all summer to put together."

He sips from his glass and watches the fire grow.

"Must've eaten up your whole savings account."

Sam glances back at him and smiles. "Just part of my half of the money we got when we sold the house."

Montgomery drinks instead of replying. He and Al never owned property together. The house they lived in was a rental.

Sam sits down on the floor in front of the fireplace, his knees up and his elbows on them. Montgomery waits a moment before crossing the room to join him. He sits down on Sam's left. He can feel the heat of the flames. They're close enough that their elbows brush whenever one of them takes a drink. They drain their glasses in silence, then Sam pours them both a second and lies down on the rug, propped on one elbow. Montgomery stays seated, his back now to Sam, staring into the fire. He can smell the pine logs collected nearby and the wood smoke. The room is warmer now, and it was a touch cool before.

Montgomery thinks about fires: the bonfire at the 4th of July party where he met Al, hundreds of campfires built throughout his ranching career, a fire on a beach in South Texas that he and Al built on a chilly night of a vacation they took, campfires he and his father built when Montgomery was a kid and they'd take off for the woods in Colorado, the fire that he and Al burned their vows in, the fire that he and Bo Davis shared one night working alone together by which light Montgomery looked at him and felt how deeply he loved his friend.

"You ever wonder how you got here?" Sam says. "Sometimes, I stop and look around and realize how far away this reality is from what I expected a few years ago. It makes me curious about the future."

"Not skeptical?" says Montgomery.

Sam pauses. "I don't think so. I don't have a plan, you know? No direction. I have a job and a place to live and some people in my life, and I don't know what else to want..... Did you ever get that feeling when you were young, that you were going somewhere and one day you'd arrive? I thought I'd arrived when I married Jen. All that was left to do was have kids. Maybe I'd be sheriff of the county one day. I don't know. Now, it's like—like I'm back on the road again but I don't have a destination."

Montgomery takes a drink and says, "If it wasn't for a couple of jackasses holding up a diner and trying to kill you, we would've never met. Could've lived half an hour apart for years, passed each other by dozens of times, and never once had reason to meet."

"I probably would've pulled you over for speeding eventually," Sam says.

Montgomery smiles, his back still to Sam. He's feeling the whiskey now, his face and his insides warmer with it. He sinks backward, stretching out next to Sam and mirroring the other man's posture, turned on his side and propped on one elbow.

After a few minutes of silence, the two of them not looking at each other as they sip their drinks, Sam speaks.

"Why did you do it?"

"Do what?"

"Why did you save my life at the diner?"

Montgomery doesn't answer right away. At the time, he wasn't doing a whole lot of thinking. He reacted to the sight of Decker threatening someone with his weapon, and it didn't make a difference whether it was a defenseless teenager or a sheriff's deputy. The whole drama happened in minutes, faster than anyone who hasn't experienced it would expect, and Montgomery did what he did because he knew that he had a chance against Decker and didn't want to see anyone hurt.

"He could've shot you," Sam says, eyes slanted toward the fireplace. "Most people wouldn't stick their neck out for a cop they don't know. Even if they had a weapon."

"You're a person," Montgomery says. "Not a job. You're a man, no different than any other man who was there that night. No different than me."

Sam looks at him, and Montgomery doesn't meet his gaze. He finishes his drink.

"Can I tell you a secret?" Sam says.

Montgomery looks at him. Sam looks about as drunk as Montgomery feels. Montgomery nods.

"I've only ever dated women, but... there have been a couple times where I thought—where I felt some kind of love for other men that might've been romantic. They were really close friends of mine, and I wanted us to be something, to be... I don't know. I've never really wanted to have sex with men. That's why I've never tried dating them." Sam pauses and takes a deep breath, blowing it out. "I think I would've liked being physical with those friends, not in a sexual way but... And I don't know if I would've wanted to actually date them, even if they were all right with a nonsexual relationship. I know I'm not making any sense, but I'm trying to say that maybe I want to explore some kind of intimacy with a man, if the right one comes along. Instead of looking for a girlfriend."

Montgomery turns his head to look at Sam, who's still staring into the fire. He's not sure what Sam means, but he knows he has to tell the truth in turn. "There's something you oughta know," he says. "About me and my wife. I loved her but I wasn't in love with her. Our marriage ended because I've never liked sex, and I got to a point where I didn't want to go through the motions anymore. She was one of my best friends, and I wanted to be with her. Just not the way she wanted to be with me."

Sam stares at him, silent and unreadable. Montgomery's relieved not to see pity or criticism in his eyes, but he's still afraid of what Sam will say. He's never told anyone the truth about his sexuality or his divorce. Not even Al fully understands.

"What do you mean, you wanted to be with her?" Sam asks, his voice now soft, softer than the fire. His eyes are glassy.

"I would've stayed married to her if I could've," Montgomery says. "Been her partner in life. Without the sex, without the romance. And maybe she could've had someone else besides me, a man who could give her those things. But we still would've been partners, you know? Family."

Sam doesn't reply or look away.

"It's a crazy idea. But she was one of my best friends. I just wish that counted for something."

Sam stares at Montgomery in silence, as if he can come to understand him that way. The whole house is dark and quiet, except for the intermittent crackling of the fire and their breathing. A little light from the stars and the moon filters through the windows at the front of the room, silvery white. Sam lays his hand on Montgomery's face, cupping his cheek. They look at each other in silence, the glow of the fire on their skin, the gleam of it in their eyes. The whiskey bottle's still between them.

"You're lonely as hell, aren't you?" Sam says.

Montgomery pauses, eyes fixed on Sam's. "I know you are," he says. He wants to cover Sam's hand with his own but he doesn't.

"How?"

Montgomery swallows. "Because here you are settling for my company."

"You're good company," Sam says.

Montgomery closes his eyes, feeling Sam's hand

on his cheek and waiting for it to slip away.

"Hey."

Montgomery opens his eyes, but they stay half-lidded, heavy with alcohol and the heat of the fire.

"I care about you," Sam says. "I want to be your friend. But if you don't want to be mine, just tell me."

Montgomery lays his hand on Sam's side, over his ribs. He's almost surprised at himself for the motion, but he doesn't pull back. "We are friends."

Sam smiles—the kind of deep, true, happy smile that reaches his eyes and glows through his whole face. His hand slides off Montgomery's face and down to cup Montgomery's neck. They continue to look at each other a minute. Montgomery wonders in the silence if Sam is going to kiss him, and he's drunk enough that he probably wouldn't care if Sam did. Staring into each other's eyes this long is almost more intimate than a kiss.

"I think I'm drunk," Montgomery says, all of his physical awareness focused into Sam's hand on his neck.

Sam huffs a laugh and drops his hand, picking up the whiskey bottle between them and holding it up. It's a little more than half-empty. "You think?" He slides the bottle away from them on the rug, and it stops just under the coffee table.

Montgomery sinks the rest of the way down, lying on his back and looking up at the ceiling. He rubs at his forehead, shading his eyes. The light of the fire blankets the length of his body, up to the collar of his flannel shirt. "What time is it?" he says.

Sam checks his watch, taking longer than usual to decipher it. "Almost one."

Montgomery breathes out through his nose, in tired resignation. "Guess I'll stay on your couch tonight if you don't mind."

"You're always welcome," says Sam, still up on his elbow and looking down at Montgomery.

For a while, Montgomery stares at the ceiling, and neither of them speak, the gentle crackling of the fire the only sound in the house. His eyes slide over to Sam eventually. Maybe it's the way Sam's looking at him or maybe it's the whiskey—but a thick, warm burst of affection expands in his chest like raw cotton fresh out of the dryer. It isn't nostalgia this time. It's for no one else but Sam.

Sam lies down on the rug next to him, and they look at each other, heads turned left and right.

Montgomery swallows, his mouth dry and his mind slow. "You ever miss having someone in your bed?" he says, his voice almost too quiet. "Just to hold onto 'n wake up with? Someone who makes you feel less alone in the world?"

Sam pauses before he nods.

Montgomery doesn't move or speak again, just keeps his eyes on Sam.

A minute passes, and Sam rolls onto his side toward Montgomery, reaching out for him. Montgomery turns to him, hugs Sam one-armed just as Sam pulls him close. Sam, the shorter of the two, fits his head below Montgomery's and against his chest. He holds onto Montgomery's waist, and Montgomery keeps his arm wrapped around Sam's back. All the tension he didn't know was there melts out of Montgomery's body, and he goes boneless on the rug, the scent of Sam's hair filling his nose as he passes out.

# CHAPTER NINE

The birds wake Sam up, singing in the early morning. It takes him a minute to remember where he is and how he got here, lifting his head up off the shag rug and looking around a little through half-open eyes. The room is dim with only the weak, gray light falling through the front window. The fire has long since died out, leaving only blackened wood and ash in the fireplace. He thinks he can feel cold air from outside seeping in through the open flue, but he's warm in yesterday's clothes, pressed up against Montgomery's broad back. They're lying on their sides facing the back of the room. Sam has his arm wrapped around the other man's chest and his knee in between Montgomery's. He looks at the back of Montgomery's head in silence, waiting to see if he stirs. He can't believe they spent the night sleeping together, cuddling. He eyes the bottle of Maker's 46 under the coffee table behind them.

Sam lies down again and carefully hooks his arm around Montgomery's waist, resting his face against the soft flannel covering Montgomery's back. It's been a long time since he and another man held each other, and there have been plenty of women since then. Holding Montgomery isn't anything like holding a woman. Sam thinks about Lauren Baker and the last time they had sex. She isn't the cuddly type, but what few times he's spooned up behind her after they screwed, she felt about the same as every other lover he's had. Smooth skin, smaller frame than his own, body soft and round, long hair that he could lace his fingers into, the smell of her subtle and feminine. Despite Sam having a stockier build, Montgomery's bigger than Sam, taller, his shoulders wider, his arms stronger. Sam can feel the muscles through Montgomery's shirt, built through physical labor outside of a gym. The lines of his body are straighter, more angular than a woman's, and he's more solid, heavier and harder. It isn't arousing to Sam, the way holding Lauren or some other beautiful woman would be. This doesn't feel sexual, cuddling with Montgomery. It feels intimate, comforting.

Sam closes his eyes. He can smell the muskiness of Montgomery's skin mixed with a clean, plain soap and cigarette smoke in his clothes. He feels the breath moving through Montgomery's body, slow and shallow. He doesn't hear anything except the birds outside.

When he wakes again, he's alone on the rug, covered in the blanket that he keeps folded on one of the sofas. He sits up, checks his watch, and looks around. He starts to feel disappointed when it seems that Montgomery left, but before he can get on his feet, Sam hears the boot heels on the kitchen floor.

Montgomery comes back to him with a mug in each hand. He offers one to Sam. Coffee.

"Thanks," Sam says, smiling. He doesn't look at Montgomery directly, now a little shy and unsure if he's supposed to pretend that they didn't sleep through the night cuddled up. He takes a preliminary sip to test the coffee's temperature.

Montgomery gave it to him black with what tastes like a teaspoon of sugar. Sam usually drinks it with cream.

Montgomery stands back and drinks from his own mug, looking down at Sam with the same cool demeanor he always has when he's sober. He's got his free hand on his hip, and, except for his untucked shirt, he doesn't look like he spent the night on the floor.

Sam's quiet for a while, drinking his coffee as an excuse not to speak. He hopes Montgomery will say something first, but when he doesn't, Sam decides to pick neutral ground. "You feel like breakfast?"

Montgomery, still watching him, pauses and says, "I could eat."

"We're probably better off going someplace," Sam says, trying to think about what he has in his kitchen.

Montgomery sips on his coffee. "I think I can come up with something here, if you don't mind."

Sam blinks at him, his mug warm against the backs of his fingers. "You want to cook?"

Montgomery doesn't quite smile. "If the food's not up to your standards, you don't have to eat it," he says. "Promise."

Sam sits at the kitchen table while Montgomery cooks, quiet as he ponders what to say. He finishes his coffee and looks at Montgomery's back, which stays turned to him for most of the forty-five minutes it takes to make breakfast. Montgomery doesn't say a word either during that time. Sam finds the silence between them comforting instead of awkward, something about the atmosphere of the house now on this Sunday morning with just the two of them together. He starts thinking about what it'd be like if this happened more often, if Montgomery lived with him, if they shared a bed every night and started every day together like this in the kitchen, if Sam knew that he'd have a friend to come home to after work every evening.

He tenses as he catches himself, goes to drink more coffee to calm his nerves but his mug's empty.

Montgomery sets the two plates of food on the table and brings the coffee pot over from the counter. He sits across from Sam and sips at his own mug. Sam pours himself a refill, not looking at Montgomery now.

Breakfast is scrambled eggs with cheese, diced potatoes roasted brown, and biscuits from a can with butter. Nothing fancy but it tastes good. The two men eat in silence until they're both about halfway done.

"Listen," Montgomery says, looking up at Sam with his clear, dark eyes. "Last night was all right, but I don't want to give you the wrong impression. I don't know how much you understood 'bout what I was trying to say..."

He pauses, and Sam watches him, taken off guard by the sting of disappointment he feels, thinking he's about to get rejected. He's still not sure what he wants beyond some kind of closeness, but it sounds like Montgomery's about to turn him down anyhow.

"I know you said you don't want to have sex with men," Montgomery continues. "But if you're looking for a boyfriend... That's not something I can be. It's not something I can do. But I like being friends with you, Sam. I hope that makes sense."

Sam pauses and swallows, his mouth dry and his hands clammy. "I like being friends with you, too," he says, then tries to smile. "I'm not looking for a boyfriend. I don't know what I'm looking for."

He peers down into his mug, both his hands around the base now. He takes a breath, feels Montgomery's eyes on him, and looks back up.

"It was nice, spending the night with you."

Montgomery doesn't answer right away. "Yeah?" he says.

Sam nods. "This is, too. Breakfast."

Montgomery doesn't reply, and after a quiet moment, he goes back to his food.

Sam follows his lead, but he wants to know if Montgomery agrees with him. He's afraid to hear "no," so he keeps his mouth shut.

Montgomery pours himself a little more coffee and says, without looking at Sam, "If you ever want to do this again some time, on a weekend, all you gotta do is ask."

Sam can't help but freeze and stare at him, unsure if he heard right.

Montgomery sips his coffee, glances at Sam, and resumes eating.

Sam decides not to reply.

When their plates are clear, Sam rinses them in the sink and puts them in the dishwasher, while Montgomery steps out to smoke. Sam picks one his jackets from the coat rack by the front door and puts it on before going out to join him.

The birds are quiet now, the sky a little brighter. Montgomery leans against one of the porch columns at the top of the steps, cigarette in his lips and coffee mug in one hand. Sam comes up alongside him and they look out at the neighborhood together. It's chilly, but Montgomery doesn't seem uncomfortable without the jacket he left inside.

"So," Sam says, calmer now that he's out of the kitchen. "You coming to Thanksgiving?"

Montgomery takes the cigarette from his lips and brings his mug up to drink. "Maybe," he says.

They stand there together until the cigarette's smoked down to the filter and the coffee's lukewarm at the bottom of the mug.

*~*~*

Monday morning, Montgomery drives out to Dewey-Humboldt with his gun on the bench seat next to him. He takes the same route he took once before, through the town proper and east into the rural outskirts of scattered homes and loner RVs. This time, he goes straight down the long dirt driveway and parks in front of the Airstream, gets out of his truck and notes the other one there, knocks on the camper door and waits.

Joel Troutman answers in his boxer shorts with a knife in his hand.

Montgomery's got his gun at his hip, pointed at Troutman's belly. His first cigarette of the day's still hanging from his lips, and he talks around it. "Howdy," he says.

"Who the fuck are you?" Troutman says, the look of small prey in his eyes.

"Why don't you take a step back and let me in. We'll talk."

Troutman hesitates but only for a moment. In

that moment, Montgomery figures this could go either way—smooth or bloody—depending on how wound up Troutman is. The gun Troutman brought to the diner must be here somewhere, unless it's in his truck. Even if Troutman only has that knife, Montgomery's aware of the risk of cornering him inside the Airstream. He's worked with animals long enough to know that the more confined they feel, the more skittish they are when approached and the more harm they can do to a man. But he doesn't want to make it easy for Troutman to run or be seen here with him, on the off chance that somebody else stops by before Montgomery leaves.

Troutman retreats into the camper, and Montgomery follows him inside, leading with his gun and shutting the door behind him.

Troutman sits on the couch, holding the knife in his fist on his knee, and Montgomery stays on his feet just before the door.

"Who are you?" Troutman asks again. "What do you want?"

Montgomery's eyes roam around the interior, before settling on Troutman. "You don't remember?"

Troutman stares at him for thirty seconds before the agitation in his face melts into surprise. "Holy shit. You're the guy from the diner. The one who killed Ed!" He jumps to his feet but doesn't advance toward Montgomery.

Montgomery blinks at him, his gun down at his thigh now but his finger still curled around the trigger. "I wouldn't get too excited," he says. "I killed Ed, and I'm not above killing you if I have to."

"You son of a bitch," Troutman says, a touch of

fear in his widened eyes. He doesn't move. "You murdering son of a bitch."

"Sit."

After a pause, Troutman sinks back down onto the couch.

Montgomery stands with the door at his back and watches Troutman, sizes him up proper and determines that he isn't looking at much. "Let's get something clear," he says. "Your buddy Ed got his own dumb ass shot because he was a hothead about to kill a sheriff's deputy. That's not what the two of you came to do that night in the diner, but he was fixing to do it. Fixing to kill an unarmed man of the law just because he could. That's the kinda person Ed was, but I don't reckon that's the kind you are."

Troutman stares at him with a sheen of sweat on his face, the whites of his eyes gleaming in the dimness. He doesn't reply.

"I know about your wife," Montgomery tells him. "Your boy. I know about Donna, too. I know those women ain't heard from you since the robbery. Here you are, holed up in the middle of nowhere, stalling. You're scared. You don't want to leave your family, but you know if you stay, you're going to get caught. You have been caught, Joel. Sheriff's Department knows where you are. They're coming for you. Soon. They got your plate numbers; they know what you drive."

Montgomery's speaking softer now, the way he might talk to a cow just before he kills it. The weight of the gun in his hand feels good. Heavy and warm.

"Best thing you can do is turn yourself in."

Troutman scowls at him, like the suggestion's

insulting.

"You turn yourself in now, I might just give a statement saying you didn't want Ed to kill that sheriff's deputy," Montgomery says. "That'll help you when it comes to the length of your sentence."

"Fuck you," says Troutman, now as defiant as he is tense. "I'm not going to prison."

Montgomery lowers his chin, gives Troutman a hard look. "Oh, I think you are. The only thing you have left to choose is how you go."

"I can still take my family and leave. Go across state lines. The county sheriff's department isn't going to waste their time chasing me that far."

Montgomery shakes his head. "If you were going to do that, you'da done it by now. You ain't got shit to offer'em, no way to protect'em, and even if you did, pretty sure Willa Rae isn't going to go on the run with that baby for you."

Troutman just glares at him without replying, probably because he knows Montgomery's right. He's still got the knife tight in his grip, pointing up at the ceiling on his right knee. It's a hunting knife— Montgomery's familiar with the type—and it must be sharp enough to skin.

"I don't think I have to tell you, Joel, that I could ride with you to the sheriff's station in Prescott with this gun pointed at you the whole way. I don't think you want that, and neither do I. But I'll do what I have to, if you're going to be difficult."

"What do you care if I turn myself in?" Troutman says. "You said the cops know where I am. They're coming for me. So why the hell would you show up, trying to force me to go to them, giving me a heads up about them coming while you're at it?"

Montgomery pauses. "Because I don't trust you not to do something stupid if they come here."

Troutman looks at him. "Is protecting the sheriff's department a hobby of yours?"

Montgomery doesn't answer. He points his gun at Troutman's chest.

Troutman tenses up, squirming into the back of the sofa. "What are you doing?"

"How 'bout I just shoot you, then call you an ambulance?" Montgomery says. "And you wake up cuffed to your bed in the hospital."

# CHAPTER TEN

Sam drives his unit behind the Prescott sheriff's lieutenant, second in a line of marked department cars. They creep along the dirt road leading to Troutman's campsite without their lights or sirens announcing them, heading for the sun-bleached bare trees. The silver Airstream glints in the distance.

Sam parks his unit behind the lieutenant's and cuts the engine. He peeks into the rearview mirror at the vehicles behind him, touches his weapon to make sure it's still there on his belt, and waits until he sees the lieutenant emerge from the SUV in front of him before getting out of his own unit.

The three other deputies present come out of their vehicles, the sound of their doors closing loud and sharp in the cold quiet of the campsite. Sam looks over his shoulder and sees them walking up the dirt path toward him, then moves up alongside the LT's unit as the older man proceeds to the Airstream.

Sam freezes next to the front end of the SUV, when he sees the familiar black pick-up truck parked ahead of it, right next to the camper. Plenty of people in this county drive old trucks like that, but Sam knows without getting closer that it's Montgomery's. His eyes fly to the camper door just as the lieutenant knocks on it.

"Yavapai County Sheriff's Department," the LT

says in a raised voice.

No response.

The LT raps his knuckles on the door again, harder this time. "Come out with your hands up or we're breaking in."

"You back off!" Troutman shouts from inside the Airstream. "I got a hostage! I got someone in here with me, and if you don't get the hell off my lot, I'll kill him."

"Who's in there with you?"

"Fuck off! Now! Or I swear to God, I'll shoot him, you hear me?"

The LT pauses, then turns around and goes down the metal steps. He walks a few paces away from the camper, the deputies watching him like a pack of well-trained dogs waiting for a signal from their master, then faces the camper again with hands on his hips. It's quiet enough in the clearing that voices carry loud and clear when shouting, so he doesn't ask anyone for a megaphone. He just hollers, "Mr. Troutman, I need you to come out with your hostage. I need to see that he's alive and well—because if he isn't and you insist on barricading yourself inside, we might just have to shoot your trailer up full of holes and count your hostage an inevitable casualty."

He's bluffing, Sam thinks as he looks back and forth from the LT's back to the silver Airstream. The deputies would hang for pulling a stunt like that, and the lieutenant's not crazy enough to order it. But Troutman might believe the lie.

"Mr. Troutman?" the LT calls.

One of the screened windows squeals open and Troutman, who remains obscured, answers. "I will fucking shoot this bastard, if you don't leave! His blood's going to be on your hands!"

"No, I don't think you will, Joel. Because if you do, we have no reason not to kill you for refusing to surrender."

Silence.

"Now come on out here with the man, show us he's still alive, and we'll deal with you," the LT says.

Nothing happens for a minute that feels like an hour.

The door pops open, hinges squeaking as it swings back, and a pair of brown cowboy boots leads a tall man outside, slouching forward to duck under the door frame.

Montgomery, his hands raised palms forward.

A few steps behind him, Joel Troutman follows with a gun. They come down off the camper steps and onto the hard, dry ground. Montgomery stops when he reaches the front end of his truck, several paces in front of the lieutenant's unit, and Troutman stops with him, the gun only about a foot from Montgomery's back.

A silence settles over the trees and the campsite like a blanket of snow. Sam hears himself suck in a breath that he doesn't exhale. None of the other deputies make a sound. Montgomery and Troutman look at them, and the deputies look back, both sides unprepared for this situation.

Sam finds Montgomery's eyes. Montgomery doesn't come off scared, but Sam sure as hell is.

"Joel Troutman," Lieutenant Warren calls out, loud enough for everyone to hear. "You're under arrest for armed robbery. Put down your weapon and no one gets hurt."

Troutman stares at the back of Montgomery's head, holding the gun steady before him. "If anybody wants this cowboy to live, you're all going to get out of the way and let me leave with him," he says, in a raised voice. "I'm not a killer. But I got at least seven rounds in this gun and I'll shoot him and as many of you as I can, if that's what I have to do."

Sam steps forward without thinking, past his lieutenant and directly across from Montgomery. He raises his hands in a placating gesture, his sidearm still holstered on his hip. "Hey," he says, his voice low and gentle. "Nobody needs to get hurt. All right? We can figure this out."

"You," Troutman says, looking at him over Montgomery's shoulder. "You're the cop from the diner."

Sam swallows and doesn't answer, maintaining eye contact with Troutman. He knows fear is all over his face, but he tells himself to stay cool-headed, tries to remember the crisis training and hostage negotiation lessons he's received half a dozen times in his career. He's already broken out in a sweat, his pulse is quick, and everything looks sharper. He thinks about how many guns there are in this showdown and how fast everything could go to hell.

"Just tell me what you want, Joel," Sam says, still holding his hands up.

"I told you," says Troutman. "You and your boys get the fuck out of my way, now. I'm leaving, and I'm taking Cowboy with me. Anybody tries to follow us or stop me, he dies."

Sam wants to look at Montgomery, but he doesn't. He gives Troutman his full attention because Troutman's the one he's dealing with.

"Mr. Troutman," the LT says, standing off to Sam's right with his hands on his hips. "I don't think I have to tell you my deputies and I are armed. We're within our legal rights to shoot you in self-defense or in defense of innocent civilians, like your hostage there. You shoot him, and you're dead."

"You going to make me shoot him?" says Troutman, smile spreading white on his face.

"No," says Sam, before the LT can reply. "Of course not. But that's the thing, Joel—if we let you go, how do we know this man will be safe?"

"I'm not a killer, I said. I got no reason to shoot him once I get clear of you."

"We're supposed to take you at your word? Do you understand why that's a tall order?"

"Sam," Montgomery says, voice soft and worn as good old boot leather.

"You shut up," says Troutman. "Make up your mind, deputy."

Sam looks to his lieutenant now, and the older man glances at him, too nonchalant.

"I'm going to have a word with my men, Mr. Troutman," the LT says. "You'll excuse us."

He turns around and disappears behind the passenger side of his SUV.

Sam meets him behind the back of the unit, the other deputies joining them in a tight huddle.

"You know who that is, Roswell?" the LT asks.

"His name's Montgomery Clark. He's a friend of mine."

"Why the hell is he here with our fugitive?"

"I don't know. But Montgomery was at the Dog Bowl the night of the hold-up. He's the one who shot Decker."

"You've got to be kidding me."

"What do we do, sir?" Deputy Beale says to the LT. "Should we call for backup?"

"You think more cops stopping up this bottleneck is going to make things better, Beale?"

"I think you should leave me with them," says Sam, looking at the LT. "If there's only one of us here, that should make Troutman feel less cornered, more in control, and he'll be able to get away if it comes to that, or at least believe that he can."

"Are you out of your mind, Roswell? I didn't come here to let this jackass get away. And if you think I can leave one deputy alone with an armed fugitive who's taken a hostage, you should see somebody about your mental health."

Sam raises his voice now, an edge of desperation to it, looking at his commanding officer as if no one else is there. "Sir, our primary objective now is to secure the hostage alive and uninjured. If we let Troutman leave with him, we lose control of the situation. If all five of us stand our ground and try to intimidate Troutman into surrendering, there's a real risk that somebody gets hurt, maybe even killed. I think I can get Troutman to release the hostage if I'm the only one he's gotta face, and once that happens, you can chase him to kingdom come and use all necessary force without hesitation."

The lieutenant stares at Sam for a silent pause, his expression surly. "Fine," he says. "Have it your way. But if this goes belly up, you'll answer to the sheriff and take full responsibility."

"Yes, sir."

"You got your sidearm, Roswell?"

"Yes, sir," Sam says, touching the gun in his hip holster.

"Don't be conservative about using it," the lieutenant says.

All of the sheriff's deputies climb back into their units. The vehicles behind Sam's move slowly in reverse down the dirt path away from the campsite. Sam moves his unit off to the left, past the mouth of the path and into the circular clearing. He gets out again and rounds the vehicle to watch the lieutenant go. The lieutenant turns his unit around, idles for a moment, rolls down his window and gives Sam a last look. The kind of look a disappointed father gives his adolescent son before taking off.

Once he's alone, Sam goes to face Troutman and Montgomery. The sun's higher in the sky now, the light brighter and flashing in every metal surface it touches: the Airstream, the pickup trucks and their silver trim, Sam's unit, the gun in Troutman's hands, and the star pinned onto Sam's uniform. All three men have their eyes narrowed, almost squinting in the brightness. Montgomery isn't wearing his hat, Sam realizes.

"What are you still doing here, man?" Troutman asks.

"All I want is your hostage, Joel," Sam says, keeping his voice steady. "You give him to me, and we'll leave. You can hit the road after us."

"You think I'm stupid? You think I don't know you and your sheriff buddies are just going to wait for me on the highway? Or maybe I wouldn't even get that far. Maybe you'd just pull your gun on me yourself, the second I give up the cowboy."

"The other deputies are gone. They're not going to put me and your hostage in danger. And I'm telling you, I'm not trying to screw you over. I just want to get this man out of here safe. That's all."

"Bullshit," Troutman says. "No, I'm keeping him until I'm clear of you and the other cops. I think I made myself pretty fuckin' clear. So you can either turn around, get back in your car, and leave—or I'll shoot you and run with him. Your choice."

Montgomery's watching Sam with his mouth set in a hard line.

"I'm not letting you go with the hostage," Sam says. "So maybe—you take me with you. Two hostages. And you drive my car because nobody's going to stop you in a sheriff's department vehicle."

Montgomery's face remains stony and inscrutable, but there's a flinch in his eyes.

Troutman contemplates the proposal, then says, "Put your gun on the ground and kick it over here."

"Sam," Montgomery says, his tone a warning.

"You shut up, unless you want to get shot!"

Sam reaches for his pistol, keeping his eyes on Troutman, and slowly pulls it from the holster. For a split second, he considers taking the shot at Troutman. He remembers that afternoon in Skull Valley, when he and Montgomery practiced shooting empty jars and beer cans. He's not good enough. He's not going to risk Montgomery's life.

He bends down and lays the gun on the ground, then kicks it just enough to send it skidding across the yard between him and Montgomery. It stops off to the side of Montgomery's right boot.

Troutman starts to move around Montgomery, stepping sideways and aiming the gun at his head now. Sam watches, standing still with his hands up in front of him. Troutman picks up Sam's sidearm, keeping his gun pointed at Montgomery with his other hand, and throws it at the trees to the left of the Airstream. He looks over his shoulder at Sam with sinister eyes. The gun in his hand glints when it catches the sun.

"All right," Sam says. "Why don't we get in the car now?"

He reaches into his left pants pocket for the keys, keeping his other hand raised, and lifts them up to show Troutman.

"Take them. Let's go."

Troutman stares at Sam for a long, silent beat.

Sam tosses the keys at Troutman's feet.

Troutman looks at Montgomery, still pointing the gun at his head.

He whips around and shoots Sam.

Montgomery pounces on Troutman, throwing all his weight into the other man, and they tumble onto the ground. The gun goes off a second time. Troutman loses his grip on the weapon, and they scramble for it, limbs flailing, Montgomery trying to climb over Troutman while pinning him down. Troutman's fingertips are inches from the gun. He strains his arm from the shoulder to reach it, but Montgomery won't let him budge, half straddling him with one hand pressing down between Troutman's shoulder blades. Montgomery tries to reach the gun himself but he can't without letting up on Troutman.

He pivots his body on the axis of his hips, kicks his leg out and sends the gun skidding away from them with the heel of his boot. Troutman bucks

Montgomery off his back, goes to lunge for the gun, but Montgomery grabs at his ankle and trips him to the ground again. Troutman rolls onto his back and writhes around as Montgomery climbs up his body, right hand shooting up to grasp Montgomery's throat. Montgomery punches him in the face and elbows Troutman's arm, freeing himself from the chokehold.

Sitting on Troutman's belly with his knees in the ground on either side of him, Montgomery picks Troutman's upper half off the ground with his hand curled into the collar of Troutman's shirt and hits him again, letting him drop. He starts punching him with both fists, switching back and forth from left to right. He blackens both eyes and bruises both cheeks, watches blood begin to flow from the nose and the lips begin to swell, hurts his own hands on the chin and jaw. He doesn't stop until Troutman's silent and passed out, blood in his teeth and dribbling from one corner of his mouth.

Montgomery looks down at Troutman, his chest heaving for breath, neck gleaming with sweat. He feels the sun warm on his back, the air still cool on his skin. His hands stay balled into fists, arms bent at the elbows. His knuckles are raw with abrasions, fingers red and sore. He could keep beating Troutman, until the man's as good as dead. He could slit his throat with the knife. He could go get the gun and shoot him in the head like broken livestock. He could do anything now and invent a story to explain it later. The sheriff's department would believe him. Sam would forgive him.

He takes a breath and opens his hands. Stands up and steps over Troutman's immobile form.

Montgomery stumbles over to Sam, dropping to his knees beside him. Sam lies still on his back, squinting up at the bright sky, his whole left shoulder soaked in dark blood. Blood stains the ground beneath him. Blood dulls the shine of his gold sheriff's deputy star. His breathing is shallow. The pain radiates out from the entry wound into his chest and down his arm, worse than he could've imagined, more intense than any pain he's ever felt. He's sweating, his face slick with perspiration, but he's cold, as much from shock as blood loss.

"Shit," Montgomery says, leaning over Sam and looking into his eyes. "Sam? Can you hear me? Talk to me, Sam."

Sam swallows, his mouth bone dry. He feels nauseous and light-headed. He wants to speak, but he doesn't think he can. He moves his right hand on the ground a little, wanting to touch Montgomery.

"Listen, I'm going to go get you some towels. I'll be right back. I promise I will. Don't you go to sleep, Sam."

Montgomery disappears from Sam's view, and Sam's alone for what's probably only a couple minutes that feel longer. He thinks about reaching into his pocket for his cell phone, but even using his right hand to do that seems like it could spike his pain. He wants to call his lieutenant or one of the other deputies instead of 911, ask them to come back and help him if they can.

Montgomery returns with a clean towel from inside the Airstream that he folds up and presses to Sam's wound. Sam moans, almost shouting, the pain flashing white through his eyes and erupting through his body like a lit sparkler.

"I know," Montgomery murmurs, shading Sam from the sun. "Sorry."

Sam wishes he would pass out, but he can tell that isn't going to happen in the next few minutes. He doesn't know how bad the gunshot wound is, doesn't want to look at it, but he assumes he's going to live. He's not scared of dying, but he would give anything for pain relief, whether it's drugs or unconsciousness.

"Did the bullet go through?" Montgomery asks, talking in a low tone like Sam can't handle noise. "Sam?"

Sam swallows again, determined to answer, and coughs as he gets the word out. "No."

"All right. I called you an ambulance, should be here any minute. You're going to be fine."

Montgomery starts to pet Sam's hair with his free hand, crouched beside him and looking at him. Sam closes his eyes, soothed by the other man's touch.

"I'm sorry," Montgomery whispers.

Sam, who feels like he's drifting away from the world and his body with each passing minute, wants to tell him that it's Sam who's supposed to protect civilians like Montgomery. He wants to tell Montgomery that this isn't his fault. But instead, he just opens his eyes again and looks up into the other man's face, clear blue sky behind it.

Sam's not sure at first, but he thinks he can hear the whine of sirens in the distance. He wants to ask if Troutman is dead or alive, wants to know what Montgomery did to him, wants to know if Montgomery's hurt. But all he can do is lie there and look at him until his eyes won't stay open anymore.

# CHAPTER ELEVEN

Around three o'clock on Thanksgiving Day, Sam's lying in his hospital bed, watching the *Charlie Brown* holiday special that airs every year on cable. He used to watch it on TV when he was a kid, and it makes him smile with nostalgia now. He forgot all about it until his nurse, who's visited him more often than necessary today, mentioned it offhand. She feels sorry for him, he can tell. When she told him that her shift ends at five, she sounded apologetic, even though she's got a husband and two kids at home with whom to have dinner.

Sam's not unhappy, even if he should be. He spoke to his mother on the phone this morning, and to his sister and eight year old nephew. Lauren stopped by and spent a few hours with him, complete with a bottle of whiskey that she smuggled in and drank straight from after Sam declined to share it with her. Even now that he's alone, it's hard to feel blue when he's got so many bouquets to look at, along with a cluster of GET WELL SOON balloons and a teddy bear that sits on his bedside table. Every other deputy at his station, his lieutenant, his captain, and the sheriff himself have all visited over the last three days, some of them with their wives in tow bearing the flowers, and he's seen Jethro Beauty, Lauren, the guy who sells him beer at the liquor store, and a few others from around town who don't know him well. His ex-wife Jen called the day after the shooting to check on him. He didn't expect people to care so much.

Sam looks away from the television when somebody knocks on his open door.

Montgomery.

Sam smiles.

"Hey," Montgomery says, lingering in the doorway. He's gripping a canvas bag by the straps in one hand.

"Hey," says Sam. "What are you doing here?"

Montgomery comes into the room, pulls one of the chairs up close to the left side of the bed, and sits down with the bag in his lap. "Brought you food from the Barbee table. Apparently, it's Thanksgiving."

"You don't say."

"I know it ain't dinner time, so if you're hungry again later, I can find you something else."

Montgomery takes the two big Tupperware containers out of the bag, sets one on the tray that folds out of Sam's bed, passes Sam silverware and napkins, and puts the second container in his lap. He lays a bunch of biscuits folded up in a cloth napkin on the bed in front of him.

"How you feeling?" he says.

"The same," says Sam, lying there without touching the container of food or utensils. "Which isn't bad. They still got me up to my eyeballs in painkillers."

"Enjoy it while it lasts. Once they send you home, you'll have to get along with pills, and even the prescription kind ain't as good as whatever's in that drip."

"I'm not complaining, but I think I'm about ready

to get out of here."

Montgomery gives Sam a skeptical look and reaches for a biscuit.

The damage to Sam's left shoulder is serious, and while the surgery to remove the bullet and repair the tissue was successful, he's in for a long recovery. He was fortunate enough to escape bone and nerve trauma, which would've made things significantly worse, but he's looking at months of rehab with no guarantee of regaining perfect function and mobility in the shoulder. The doctor told him he'll need prescription pain meds for at least part, if not all, of his recovery time. His left arm's out of commission for the foreseeable future, which means he'll need help with basic tasks during the next several weeks. He's on paid medical leave from work until further notice, but even when he's ready to go back, he'll be office bound until he meets the department's standard of physical fitness—if he ever does. Being right-handed, he can still use his gun, which increases his chances of field reinstatement, but if he has a permanent disability, his law enforcement career is all but over, unless he wants to take an administrative position.

It's too much to think about now, and he's been ignoring it most of the time, since waking up from surgery three days ago. He's just glad that he's alive, that Montgomery's unharmed, and that as far as gunshot wounds go, his is non-life threatening. Sam's always been good at looking on the bright side, and this is one of those situations where the skill comes in handy.

"What the hell are you watching?" Montgomery says, looking at the TV set. "*Charlie Brown*?"

"It's the Thanksgiving special," says Sam, smiling.

"You're not a football man?"

"Nah. Not really."

"Me neither. Though I have been known to watch a Cowboys game, on occasion."

"Wait, that's right. You're from Texas. How are you not crazy about football?"

"Always been partial to the rodeo," Montgomery says. "And high school football's a bigger deal statewide in Texas than the NFL anyway."

Sam grins. "Were you on the team? In high school?"

"Nope. Were you?"

Sam snorts. "Do I look like a football player to you?"

"No," Montgomery says, looking at Sam with a sudden soft affection in his eyes and his face.

Sam looks back at him, caught off guard by the other man's expression.

Montgomery ducks his head and pops the lid off his container of food, placing it on the bed.

Sam redirects his gaze to the TV, not knowing what to make of the moment. He still doesn't touch his food on the fold-out tray table. He doesn't want to be rude, but he doesn't have much of an appetite. He glances at Montgomery's food, then back at the TV. "What did Mrs. Barbee send you away with?" he asks.

Montgomery clears his throat and says, "Turkey, mashed potatoes, little bit of cranberry sauce, stuffing, and some green beans."

"She a good cook?"

"You tell me."

Sam doesn't reply. He doesn't move to start eating either. He watches the television for half a minute, then looks at Montgomery again and says, "I have questions. About what happened with Troutman."

Montgomery gives him an uneasy expression. "I don't know if it's a good idea, talking about all that when you're healing up."

"I'm fine. Really."

"All right," Montgomery says, after a pause. "What do you want to know?"

"Why did you go there alone? Why didn't you tell me you were going to talk to him?"

"Because I knew you'd have objections and I didn't want you there. I didn't want you in harm's way."

Sam softens at that and doesn't reply.

Montgomery continues: "I went to see if I could convince him to turn himself in. You told me that the Sheriff's department was going to go get him soon, and I didn't want that to turn into a situation if he decided to fight you. I figured if I could convince him to turn himself in peacefully, it'd be a whole lot easier for everybody."

Sam shakes his head. "I could've told you the odds of a guy like him agreeing to do that were crap."

"Yeah. I guess I should've known better. I thought I'd go there and scare him and if it didn't work, I'd just walk away and let you and your boys deal with him. I didn't think I'd end up being the reason for the whole thing going sideways. Been feeling pretty stupid about it."

"Don't," says Sam. "You had good intentions, even if they were misguided."

Montgomery hangs his head and runs a hand through his hair.

"How did you end up a hostage?" Sam asks. "That was your gun he had on you, wasn't it?"

Montgomery nods and swallows. "I threatened him when he refused to turn himself in. He still wouldn't listen, so I decided to leave. Something I said must've got to him—because when I turned my back and started out the door, he jumped me with his knife. Pushed me out of the camper. We wrestled around outside. I was trying to fight him off, trying to take the knife away from him, and somewhere in there I lost the gun. He picked it up. I think maybe I dropped it on purpose, just so I wouldn't kill him." Montgomery pauses. "I wasn't sure if I could get away with that. Or if I wanted to."

Sam's looking at Montgomery with all the focus he can muster, his shoulder throbbing through the haze of morphine.

"I don't know why he attacked me," Montgomery continues. "Why he didn't just let me leave and take off after. Maybe he wanted to show me something, after I threatened to shoot him. Maybe he was just pissed off I killed Ed Decker. I guess I can't blame him for wanting revenge. I'd want it, too, if someone killed a friend of mine."

He looks up, right into Sam's eyes.

Sam maintains eye contact until he can't stand the vulnerability of it anymore, then looks away and wrinkles the blanket and sheet in his hands.

"Anyway," Montgomery says. "He took me back into the camper once he had the gun. I don't know what he would've done if you hadn't shown up when you did. I don't think he knew either."

Maybe it's the morphine, but Sam feels almost sick as his throat tightens and his stomach clenches. He doesn't speak because he's afraid of choking. The image of Montgomery dead in that Airstream, his head blown open and his blood on the wall, flashes through his mind. He remembers the terror he felt when Troutman had that gun pointed at Montgomery, right in front of him. The dream he had weeks ago, of Troutman killing Montgomery in the diner.

After a minute filled only with the sounds of *Charlie Brown*, Montgomery says, "I been doing a lot of thinking since Monday."

"Yeah? That makes one of us," says Sam, his voice raw and raspy. He smiles a little, trying to make light of the situation. He's spent most of the last three days unconscious.

Montgomery pauses. "When we were out there at Troutman's hideaway, waiting for the deputies to come back, I'm pretty sure I knew you were going to live—but there was a split second, right after Troutman shot you, I didn't know where you'd been hit. I didn't have time to dwell on it because I had to get him, but I felt... well, I can't really put into words how I felt. And then once you were here and they took you in to surgery and I had hours to myself, I kept wishing it was me in your place."

Sam's looking right at him now, and Montgomery's looking back, grey eyes and blue holding each other steady.

"I figured you'd make it," Montgomery says. "But I didn't want you to be in pain. Still don't."

Sam swallows, his throat tight with emotion. He doesn't even try to speak because he knows he'll choke up if he does, and he can't think of anything to say anyway.

"Maybe if I hadn't gone out there when I did, none of this would've happened, and if that's true, I'm sorry. You gettin' hurt is part on me. That's one thing I've wanted to say the last few days."

"What else?" Sam says, his voice hoarse and quiet.

Montgomery looks away from him, down and off to his left. He doesn't answer at first, and Sam waits, watching him. Sam takes in the softness of Montgomery's face, the lines creased into his skin at the corners of his eyes, the weather worn skin still young and clean shaven for once. It was violence and death that brought them together in the first place, and Montgomery was the most vivid part of the most traumatic experience of Sam's life.

But Sam doesn't want to see him that way. When he closes his eyes and thinks of Montgomery, he doesn't see a man with a gun in his hand. He doesn't see blood or feel pain. He sees the cowboy on a horse in the desert. He sees him in a field with the mountains behind him, the sky dusty pink with sunset. The last good and pure thing in the world, just beyond him in the distance.

"I thought I was used to being alone," Montgomery says. "But some time these last few months, I got to liking your company. Now, I don't want to go without it."

Sam stares at him, and Montgomery meets his eyes again.

"I don't know you well enough, but I want to."

Montgomery swallows. "I want to, Sam. I want—" He stops, maybe because his voice was about to crack, but he doesn't look away.

"What?" Sam says, before he can stop himself. "What do you want?"

Montgomery pauses, his gray eyes clear but the rest of him wrung out. He doesn't speak for a long minute, as if he's gathering his thoughts and trying to figure out how to express them. "You ever watch the old Westerns? The classics? You remember in a lot of those stories, the hero was a man who didn't have a family, no wife, nothing to tie him anyplace—but he had a partner, another man who rode with him? And they'd go from town to town or just stay in the nowhere between towns, looking for the next adventure and living simple in the mean time? Didn't matter if they were outlaws or cowboys or deputies. They had each other to the end."

Sam feels heavy on the bed and the pillow, lying there and looking at Montgomery. Maybe it's the opiates coursing through his body, but the weight of Montgomery's loneliness hits him like a foul ball to the gut. He finally understands the other man, even if he can't describe what he knows, and it breaks his heart some kind of way it hasn't been hurt since he was a boy.

Montgomery's looking at him with more earnestness than Sam's ever seen, waiting to hear whether or not Sam gets him.

And Sam says, "Do I get to be Butch?"

Montgomery blinks, then breaks into a God honest smile.

"Because I think you're more of a Sundance."

"Things didn't end well for those two," Montgomery says. "Maybe you should pick a different pair."

They're quiet for a little while, letting time and silence take the heat out of the conversation as their smiles fade away.

Then Sam says, "I think I could do that."

He's looking at Montgomery with warmth in his eyes, and Montgomery lifts his head to meet them.

"I think I could be your partner one day. Trade a normal life for something better with you. I'm not any good at normal anyway."

Montgomery stares at him, and Sam smiles deep and wide with the pleasure of making the decision out loud.

"I'm not asking you for anything," Montgomery says.

"I know," says Sam. "But I'm offering."

Montgomery pauses, looking not so brave or cool in the chair. "I don't think I can believe you yet. I can't trust that you won't change your mind."

"That's all right. I have time to prove myself."

Sam looks back at the TV, satisfied with the talk. *Charlie Brown's* almost over.

Montgomery sucks in a breath and stands up like he's been sitting too long and his joints are stiff. "Better find us a microwave," he says and grabs the container of food off Sam's tray table, holding his own in his other hand.

"Montgomery," Sam says.

Montgomery stops in the doorway and looks over his shoulder.

"I promise I won't hurt you."

Montgomery gives a slight nod and walks out of

the room.

Maybe he doesn't trust that either, but for the first time since he proposed to his ex-wife, Sam feels like he knows what he wants and where he's going. For the first time since his divorce, he feels like he has something to look forward to.

# EPILOGUE

They're sitting in a pair of rocking chairs on Montgomery's front porch, watching dusk stain the sky orange, pink, red, and purple. Montgomery's drinking a cold beer from the ice box on the floor between them, and Sam, who's still on prescription pain killers, has a cup of hot coffee between his thighs on the seat of his chair. They don't say much, the sound of their chairs creaking on the porch boards filling the silence.

Montgomery glances over at Sam and says, "You gettin' cold?"

"No, I'm good," says Sam, whose left arm is in a sling instead of his jacket sleeve.

"Let me know when you wanna go in."

Montgomery pulls on his beer, then sticks the bottle between his legs and lights a cigarette. The smoke smells good in the cold air, and Sam smiles to himself, content next to the other man in the beautiful remoteness of Skull Valley.

Ever since Sam got out of the hospital, Montgomery's been looking after him whenever he can, spending weeknights at Sam's house and bringing Sam to his place on weekends. He cares for Sam with the same kindness that Sam imagines him showing to the animals on Barbee's ranch, the same quiet humility. Sam didn't ask him for help, didn't expect him to do as much as he's doing, and the one time he thanked him, Montgomery told him he didn't need to hear it again.

"I've been thinking," Sam says.

"Yeah?" says Montgomery, his chair still now as he smokes.

"I've been thinking about what I'll do if I have to leave the force."

"Who says you will?"

"It's a real possibility. If my shoulder doesn't heal right, if I can't use my sidearm right, I can either take an admin position or retire. And I think I'd rather just leave if it comes to that. But I don't know what I'll do if I quit. I've been a cop since I was twenty-four. I've never really imagined anything else, all these years."

Montgomery doesn't reply for a minute, the two of them looking out at the landscape. There's snow on the mountains in the distance, but they haven't seen any yet in Skull Valley or Prescott, even though December is already half gone.

"You want to keep being a deputy?" Montgomery asks.

Sam looks at him. "Yeah."

"Then don't waste your time trying to figure out alternatives."

Sam doesn't argue.

But after a moment, Montgomery says, "I could probably make some kinda cowboy outta you, if you put your mind to it."

Fin

## About the Author

Marie S. Crosswell is a novelist, short story writer, and poet. She is a graduate of Sarah Lawrence College, where she concentrated on creative writing and friendship studies. Her short crime fiction has previously appeared in Thuglit, Plots with Guns, Flash Fiction Offensive, Beat to a Pulp, Betty Fedora, Dark Corners, and Locked and Loaded: Both Barrels Vol. 3. Her novella TEXAS, HOLD YOUR QUEENS is available from One Eye Press.

She lives in Arizona with her black cat.

CPSIA information can be obtained
at www.ICGtesting.com
Printed in the USA
BVOW06s2152291216
472229BV00001B/14/P